GRANDPA'S CABIN

BOOK 1

6/16
Thank you Chrissy!

ROSS VICTORY

Created and written by J. Ross Victory
www.rossvictory.com

Edited by Treharne O'Grady
Proofread by Liz Saucedo

Cover and chapter art illustrated by David Izaguirre, Jr.

Cover graphic design, layout, and coloring by William Sikora III
www.sikoraentertainment.com

ISBN: 979-8-218-01789-7 (paperback)
ISBN: 979-8-218-01790-3 (e-book)

www.rossvictory.com
booksandbangers@gmail.com

GRANDPA'S CABIN
BOOK 1

At eighty-four years old, widower and award-winning geneticist Bernie Crenshaw has reached the end of his life. Bernie gifts his only grandson, eighteen-year-old Inglewood high school senior Nova, his multimillion-dollar property located in Los Angeles' Hollywood Hills.

Hours before his death, Bernie informs Nova that he did terrible deeds years ago. Bernie reveals that he never got caught because his freedom was contingent on an agreement he made with a "woman in the shadows" to keep the cabin in the family's bloodline. Nova promises his grandfather that he will never sell the property.

Years after Bernie's death, Nova hosts a wild twenty-first birthday party weekend filled with alcohol, music, and OnlyFans web cameras. After a handful of eerie encounters in the surrounding Los Angeles forest, Nova's friends allege that his grandpa's cabin is the burial ground for people who disappeared during their childhood.

The birthday weekend shifts from celebration to terror as the friends piece together that the man Nova knew as "Popsi" matches the profile of one of the most notorious wanted criminals in Los Angeles—"L.A. Love Hunter."

Will Nova preserve the Crenshaw family's sadistic legacy, or will he choose the rare and valuable gift of friendship?

CONTENT NOTICE

Grandpa's Cabin is a horror story that
contains graphic descriptions, sexual
situations, and psychologically disturbing
content. The author understands the
importance of providing this notice.

CONTENTS

PROLOGUE

Fourteen years ago, Los Angeles

Nova did not understand why first grade had ended early. Dozens of armed security guards descended on the elementary school with their guns drawn. The events of the day, which started with learning to tell time on a silly-framed clock and identifying vowels in sentences, had become disjointed puzzles in Nova's six-year-old mind, a mind easily distracted by dogs' tails and why his father shaves his face, but his mother shaves her underarms. Today, his bite-sized body would experience panic, and his mind would be introduced to a modern emotion: terror.

Mr. Woodrow, a frumpy man, only thirty-five but looked sixty, paced the classroom, which was decorated in circus-themed letters and talking numbers. His face was pale and fear-stricken as he explained today's events to the officers, who observed him with deep suspicion.

"Sir, six-year-old kids don't just run away from chocolate chip cookies and story time. We need you to breathe and tell us the last time you saw the twins."

Two chairs, which had been occupied before the recess bell, were now empty. A class of twenty bright-eyed first graders was now eighteen. No one knew where the twins had gone.

After hours of waiting, the class was escorted to the pickup lot, where Nova found his mother, Stella, standing next to their black Range Rover and anxiously biting her left thumbnail down its nail plate.

"Oh, my God!" Stella burst out as she hugged Nova's frail body tightly. She kissed Nova's head repeatedly. "Are you okay? You must be so scared." Nova stood motionless and confused by his mother's panic.

Stella tapped frantically on her cellphone. "I'm calling your father." Stella began to breathe in through her nose and out through her mouth, counting to four out loud. After several failed phone calls, Stella threw her cellphone into the car, quickly ushering Nova into the back seat. They sped off in silence. "Let's go, let's go," Stella said.

Nova was always picked up by his maid or driven and escorted by their assistant, Lennox. Unaware of how privileged he was, Nova thought of the service staff as his friends and extended family to help him through his life at any given moment. Nova could sense his mother's shock from the back seat. He watched the same fear in his mother's tear-stained eyes that had just been in Mr.

Woodrow's. They briefly made eye contact through the rearview mirror before Stella slammed on the brakes, nearly hitting two pedestrians lollygagging in the crosswalk.

"Honey, I'm thinking today is a good day for ice cream. What do you say?" Stella weaved in and out of traffic away from the private elementary school toward the hills of Los Angeles, which were barely visible through the thick layer of smog covering the mountain tops like 'boo boo' brown cake icing.

"Bernie? This is Stella." Stella whispered into her phone, "Two kids were...kidnapped at Nova's school, and I can't reach your son, so I'm headed your way."

"Kidnapped?" Nova repeated to himself. "Mommy, the kids take a nap after lunch. Mr. Woodrow doesn't allow kids napping."

"Honey, quiet, please!"

Nova was confused by the set of events that led him to this point. He clutched his stuffed bunny in his arms and tinkered with his hearing aid, trying to understand what had just happened.

"Stop touching it, Nova."

Nova barely heard the words exchanged as his mother spoke to his grandfather, for he had been distracted by the slow dance of two bulbous damselflies weaving between neatly arranged flower bushes on the street corner. Stella screeched to a halt at the entrance of Grandpa

Bernie's (Popsi's) driveway as the huge gates opened. Bernie greeted Stella and Nova at the front door.

"Is that my favorite *superNova?*" Bernie asked as he hugged his grandson.

When Nova took Bernie's hand, he turned to see his mother leaving without a second glance. Nova frowned. *Why didn't she say goodbye?* He had wanted to say goodbye. Soon, his memories of the day were only distant dreams, as he splashed and played with toys in his grandfather's pool while being waited on, wish and whim, by Lennox, the non-binary family butler.

It wasn't until Nova slept that the day took on meaning, and the dark chamber of dreams shifted into lucid night terrors, affixing the crux of Nova's childhood blight.

His eyes shot open to a dark endless corridor. Through the walls, he heard voices, whispers, and shouts, alien moaning, and a high-pitched drone etching closer. Nova ran from them, fleeing through the long corridor from the echoes and melting faces that emerged from the wallpaper. He ran only to crash into a door that led into darkness. Stale, silent darkness.

He screamed to try and wake up, but the walls of voices and phantom faces only grew closer.

"Nova?" a woman's voice called out through the distance. His only option was to escape deeper into the darkness. His little body carried him down a spiral staircase, feet slipping and stumbling through the shadows that clawed at his ankles like stretching demons.

At the bottom of the staircase, a light appeared far in the distance. He ran toward it, seeking shelter. Panting, he dropped to his knees in a puddle of water as fluorescent lights flickered and buzzed. Striped suspenders laid torn in the center of the puddle.

He tried to pick them up. The suspenders melted into warm ichor blood. And then came the sound of heels on concrete.

"Nova?" a woman's voice echoed through the chamber before becoming muffled.

"Mom?"

Nova looked up pleadingly, hoping to find his mother's arms. The heels came closer. He glanced up, but what he saw was not his mother's arms. Instead, he saw a woman cloaked in shadows, beckoning him deeper into the black.

"Welcome to your destiny," the woman said, shadows unwrapping her face like scattering beetles. A sudden light revealed the woman's face. An overwhelming shock from the sight of the woman's face awakened Nova to a bed drenched in sweat with an inescapable sense of remembrance.

CHAPTER ONE

Hollywood Hills

Present day

A light and airy tide of classical music drifted through the large open rooms of the Crenshaw mansion. Nova had arrived early to air the place out, opening the large glass doors to the fresh mountain breeze rolling down the hills of Los Angeles, which carried with it the scent of wealth, homelessness, and palm trees in the desert sun.

It had been years since his grandpa had passed. Nova still couldn't believe this place was all his now. He smirked at the memory of his father's face when Grandpa Bernie's lawyer had delivered the news. Eric, his father, nearly caught on fire from fury and stormed out in a fit of rage. Eric had never been a good father, and Nova rested well knowing that there was some sort of cosmic justice in the world. Eric sure as hell deserved it.

To be honest, Nova felt strange being in the mansion alone. It still smelled of Popsi, a peculiar mix of cigars, whisky, and that familiar scent many old people carry once they get to a certain age. The smell would have to go. Nova's friends were about to arrive, and he didn't want his twenty-first birthday to start off with comments on how the place smelled like the border of death and gentleman's clubs.

He sprayed cologne into the air. The bottle was probably worth more than some cars, but he sprayed it freely. Intending to renew the mansion with youth and vitality, he could only temporarily mask the smells, and they returned after a couple of minutes. Much of Nova's nonchalant personality—over-spraying expensive cologne, throwing away uneaten gourmet dishes, etc.—was rooted in the fact that he was simply unaware of how privileged he was. Grandpa Bernie had used every moment of his life breaking through the racialized wealth gap, and, as a result, Nova could access spaces and places unavailable to ninety-nine percent of the planet.

His pocket buzzed. Nova fished his phone out and swiped it to unlock the screen.

Almost there!

"Shit!"

Nova had let the time wander by, distracted by old photographs and memories of his grandfather. And he still hadn't cleaned up most of the back rooms.

He shoved old papers and random items into a cardboard box, then rushed down to the basement. A sweet, damp, musty smell wafted up the dark stairway. Nova was about to throw the box down when a headline in the stack of papers caught his eye.

Missing: Bernadette Brown - Age 8

Nova's eyebrows furrowed as he tried to interpret his grandfather's writing on the clipping. Why would his grandpa have kept something like this? At that moment, the doorbell rang.

"Shit!"

Nova threw the box down the stairs, not caring for the safety of any of the items within. He hustled toward the oversized front door, stopping for a second to brush his fresh low taper haircut in the large hall mirror. He pulled out a bottle of pills and quickly threw one into his mouth, swallowing it dry and cringing as the lump went slowly down his throat. It had been a godsend when the psychiatrist finally prescribed a mood stabilizer that worked. He had been on Zoloft for almost six years now.

Shrugging off the hard pill inching down his throat, he adjusted his hearing aid and slid the rest of the way in his socks on the marble floor before putting on his sandals.

"Wasssupppp, y'all! Welcome!" Nova stood in the open doorway to greet his friends.

Ruben went in for a bear grip hug that always left Nova slightly sore. Nova then pulled away when Ruben kissed him on the cheek.

"Holy shit, dude. When you said mansion, I didn't realize you meant *mansion*. How big is this place?"

Ruben brushed past Nova, inviting himself into the atrium without a second glance. Ruben Becerra had played varsity football at Inglewood High School and had the muscle tone of a Greek god-like the ones you see in ancient sculptures. He was covered in tattoos of Mexican muralism, quotes, and portraits of his family. In many ways, Ruben was a stereotypical guy from L.A.—Dodgers snapbacks and jerseys, over-caffeinated, and working as an entrepreneur of marijuana sales and creating social media content. Nova had identified Ruben as a friend when Ruben beat up other kids making fun of his hearing aid when they were growing up. Sometimes Ruben was brash and inappropriate, but he was authentic. Ruben was a loyal friend that Nova knew would always have his back.

"Why is this my first time up here? Your grandpa was fucking loaded!" Ruben continued, his voice growing more distant as he ventured further in. Ruben never waited for an invitation; he always took his own liberty. His inflated sense of entitlement with honest puppy dog eyes made it so that he got away with it, most of the time. He sang loudly to hear the echo of his voice.

"Hey, Nova." Magenta winked, giving him a kiss on the cheek and a spacey hug.

As her name suggested, Magenta Kim wore bright purple braids and magenta eyeshadow. She had a cool, laidback air about her and a simple smile that made her instantly likable. If you were standing in line with Magenta, she was *going* to speak to you. She was non-judgmental, had an energy that you could feel, and was known for her otherworldly ability to roll a joint with one hand while driving—being half black and half Korean allowed Magenta to code-switch effortlessly, depending on her audience. She was hyper-aware of where she was and who she was in proximity to.

"Like my nails?" Magenta said with a playful air of feline overtones. She made the shape of a claw with her hand. Each nail was long, filed to a point, and manicured with purple sparkly nail polish. "Got them from this new spot in Koreatown called Lush," she continued.

"Damn..." Nova smiled back.

"You want a joint?" Nova went to respond, but Magenta spoke before he could. "Not a question." She winked and walked into the mansion with papers and filters already in her hand.

Nova laughed to himself, shaking his head. Ruben and Magenta were his closest friends. But it wasn't them who he was most excited to see.

"Hey, Pearl."

"Nova!"

Pearl had just shut the trunk of her brand-new Mini Cooper, the larger model with four doors, which she had received for graduating from UCLA a year early. She ran up to him and flung her arms around his neck. Nova took a deep breath in as he returned the hug. Pearl smelled of the ocean and of sweet sunlit flowers with a hint of shea butter and brown sugar.

She was probably the most down-to-earth, smart girl he had ever met. Her beauty was effortless, and her sensitivity and emotional intelligence were her hidden superpowers. Pearl had bright cocoa brown eyes that sparkled with life as Nova spoke, eyes that perfectly matched the hue of her sun-kissed curls.

"Happy birthday," she whispered, still hugging him closely. "La Cienega was a nightmare! Two hours to go ten miles...only in L.A. I'm so disgusted."

Nova was about to reply when Ruben's voice cut through the moment like a brick through glass.

"Yo, Nova, what the fuck are you listening to? Cabron?!" Ruben shouted from somewhere deep in the mansion.

Ah shit. Nova had forgotten to change the classical music before everyone arrived.

Pearl released the hug and took a step back, meeting Nova's eyes with a shyly confident smile. The music quickly changed in the background, and a loud trance beat blared through the house.

"Turn that shit down," Magenta yelled from somewhere inside. "Unless it's City Girls or Nicki, it doesn't matter to me..."

Nova rolled his eyes, and Pearl laughed. "I thought Chopin was nice," Pearl said softly.

Nova was taken aback that she recognized the nineteenth-century Polish composer. She gave him a knowing look.

"Well, shall we?" Nova gestured in the entranceway.

Pearl smiled and stepped in, leaving Nova to close the door, take a big breath, and ready himself for the weekend.

Ruben and Magenta had already taken up residence in the large living room that opened into the pool area, the view from which was out over all the Los Angeles hills and city lights. Ruben had begun setting up his OnlyFans lighting and filming equipment. He was already shirtless and snapping a selfie for his Instagram, while Magenta was peering at a framed medal on the wall.

"Damn, Nova," she said as he entered, taking a puff from an expertly rolled joint. "You never told me your grandpa was a freemason."

"A what?" Nova walked up, leaning over her shoulder to see what she was talking about.

Magenta had a particular affinity for the occult and esoteric. "A freemason...probably a Prince Hall freemason," she repeated. "Prince Hall is for the black ones. It's like a secretive order. Pretty much every president was a freemason—Washington, Roosevelt." She waved her hand to suggest the list went on.

"Hmm," Nova said, surprised. "I had no idea."

Magenta took another hit, then handed the joint over to Nova. "I heard they do all sorts of strange rituals," she said. "That eye pyramid on our money is some freemason shit. Illuminati and all that. Looks like Papa was the highest of the highest. Thirty-third degree."

"Enough with all that conspiracy shit," Ruben said, walking up to them and taking the joint from Nova's hand.

Meanwhile, Pearl was outside by the pool, soaking in the view of the city.

"We got you a birthday present," Ruben said with a mischievous smile.

"Really?" Nova raised his eyebrows in surprise.

Ruben dug into his pocket and placed a small item nonchalantly in Nova's hand. Nova looked down to see a small baggie of pink, diamond-shaped pills, and at least a dozen squares of rainbow-colored paper.

"Straight from Amsterdam," Ruben said with a smile, taking a huge puff of the joint, stretching out his arms, and turning to face the pool.

"We have an awesome weekend ahead of us."

Nova agreed, but he was disappointed by Ruben's gift. *Pills? What the fuck.*

The music was still blaring, turned down slightly at Magenta's protest. But there was no question about the dynamics of the group. Ruben had always been the alpha, and things always seemed to go in his direction. At least, that's what Ruben liked to think. Magenta was always there to challenge him. And, more often than not, *her*

14

word was final. Despite her calm demeanor, Magenta had a way of commanding a room. It was her sly negotiations that would get them without fail into exclusive nightclubs and her connections that provided the entertainment on nights out in L.A.'s popular venues.

Nova and Pearl had their passivity in common. Nova was easily negotiated into illegal and dangerous antics that he had never heard of, while Pearl brought logic and caution that kept the group out of trouble. They were nowhere near as outward with their personalities, more than happy to take the backseat and allow the other two to battle out which DJ they saw or where the next road trip would be. They were also the ones who added relaxing activities to the group's agenda and, of course, drove everyone home when all was said and done.

Pearl leaned against the large glass doors to the pool, her clothes neatly folded in a small pile on the wooden deck. Nova could barely keep his eyes from noticing the curves of her body as she stood there in her white bikini.

"Who's up for a swim?" she asked.

"Yes, finally someone with some sense!" Ruben replied.

He handed the joint to Magenta and stripped down to his birthday suit.

"Ruben! I didn't mean skinny dipping—oh my God! Ewww!" Pearl continued.

"You should be glad I'm not charging you for a peep," Ruben said, chuckling.

Magenta shrugged and stripped down to her underwear. There was a loud splash as Ruben jumped in, and Nova smiled, throwing off his shirt and joining them. The sky glowed orange as the Los Angeles sun began to set, casting the clouds into soft wisps of cotton candy pink. And Ruben's trance music accompanied the sounds of splashes as Nova's birthday weekend began.

CHAPTER TWO

The Hounds

Fourteen years ago

"There's my grandson!" Bernie Crenshaw smiled as Nova and his mother, Stella, walked the distance from the car to the front door of the mansion, hand in hand.

"Hey, Bernie," Stella said somberly.

Bernie's facial expression shifted as he noticed Nova's wet cheeks and puffy eyes. "What's wrong? Where's Eric?"

Stella sighed. "He is in another one of his moods today. We didn't have the best morning..."

She continued, "Thank you for taking Nova."

Nova buried his face in the fabric of his mother's skirt.

"Oh, it's no trouble at all," Bernie said, keeping his voice optimistic and turning his attention toward his grandson. "I would bend down to hug you, but my knees aren't what they used to be. I may get stuck down there. How about we ask Lennox to scoop us up some ice cream? Aye? How does that sound?"

Nova looked up toward his grandfather and nodded with tears still in his eyes.

"Here, come on." Bernie extended his weathered hand.

Nova shifted his eyes up to seek his mother's approval. She smiled the best she could and gave him a little nudge. Nova released his grip on Stella's leg, took his grandpa's hand, and smiled.

"There you go. Why don't you run inside and get into your swim trunks, and we can practice a bit? Oh, and I have something special for you," Bernie coaxed.

Nova's eyes lit up, but only slightly. He disappeared into the walls of the mansion. Walls that were so much bigger at that age. Bernie waited until Nova was out of earshot before he looked back at Stella.

"What has my bastard son done now?" Bernie's demeanor shifted from pleasant to irritated.

Stella let out a ragged breath.

"Nothing we haven't seen before..."

Silence filled the mansion as Nova giggled in the background.

Stella sighed. "Thank you again for taking Nova. I'm just so..."

"Anytime," Bernie assured. "The boy's great company." Bernie sat down in his large French Parlor grandfather chair and searched the side table for a cigar.

Stella continued, "I'm just so..."

"What's in your heart, dear?"

"With all these missing kids in the news, I'm just so freaked out. Another little girl went missing. Same school."

Stella continued, "The news is calling this creep the *L.A. Love Hunter.*"

"*Love Hunter*, huh?"

"Is it okay if I leave Nova with you for the rest of the weekend until things calm down?"

Stella smiled, her eyes filling up with motherly love that was quickly tainted by the memory of the morning's events and fight with Eric. Bernie scanned her body language and observed the micro-expressions on her face.

"Oh, Stella..." Bernie said, taking her hand in his. "I know I shouldn't be saying this, being Eric's father and all...but, hun, don't you think it's time?"

"Time for?"

"For a divorce."

Bernie could see the emotions welling in her throat.

"Is this really about the L.A. Hunter on TV, or is it about your marriage?" Bernie continued gently.

Stella was a woman of poise and decorum. She was born to be a mother and destined to marry someone rich.

She was nurturing, supportive, and a natural problem solver. But she had an aura about her that had begun to dim. Stella had sacrificed her dream to be a lawyer to marry the man of her dreams, Eric. Over the years, Eric had shifted from the man of her dreams to the man of her nightmares. Bernie could detect Stella's unwillingness to leave his son and knew she didn't have the courage.

"Don't you worry about lawyers and money now. You will get everything you need. Perhaps then you can go back to school or start your own business? You owe yourself your own identity. I'm sure you have aspirations?" Bernie paused.

He continued, "But happiness...I rarely see happiness on your face. Eric...the man is not the same boy I raised. And I know some of it's my fault. But when does a man shift from being a victim of his circumstances to a creator of his own demise?" Bernie sighed. "Sometimes, divorce can be a positive step in both people's lives. Madeline and I thought about it a few times."

Stella offered an uncomfortable smile and turned away before Bernie could see the single tear escape her eye. Stella had wanted to leave Eric for years—years before the abuse consisted of tantrums of anger and emotional violence. Bound by tradition and duty, Stella accepted Eric as he was, believing he was going through a phase and would return to the man she once knew.

"Go and take the rest of the day off," he said. "Don't worry, *superNova* can stay for as long as he wants."

She waved goodbye from inside her car and disappeared around the bend of the driveway a moment later, the sound of tires crunching as they passed over the gray stone gravel, then the large Crenshaw gates slammed closed behind her.

* * *

"Popsi? Why do people do bad things?" Nova asked, his upper lip sticky with chocolate ice cream.

Bernie paused before answering, "Is this about your dad?"

Nova frowned and shook his head no. "Mom says Dad just gets stressed, and he doesn't mean to yell."

Bernie nodded, taking a sip of whiskey. "Then what's on your mind, my boy?"

"We had an assembly in school." Nova took another lick of ice cream. "Mr. Woodrow said James and Quinn were kidnapped."

Bernie stumbled over the fumes of his drink as the words left Nova's mouth. It took Bernie a moment to recover, but Nova was too busy with his ice cream to notice the expression on his grandpa's face.

"Kidnapped? How dreadful," Bernie finally replied. "What else did Mr. Woodrow say?"

"That we shouldn't speak to strangers and always stay with an adult."

"Wise words."

"But I don't like adults," Nova said between licks. "Except for you and Mommy." He added.

"Did you know the boys from your class well?" Bernie asked from the rim of his glass.

Nova shook his head. "No. They were weird. They were twins, and they never said anything."

"When someone is different from you, that doesn't make them weird. They are just different than *you,* understand?" Nova nodded in agreement. Bernie continued, "And don't worry yourself. I'm sure they will turn up."

"Mr. Woodrow said they went missing at the playground. The police found one of their suspenders. They always wore the same striped suspenders. Almost every day. I don't think they would just leave them there..." Nova's voice trailed off mid-sentence. "Where do you go when you get kidnapped?"

Bernie shook his head and rose from his seat by the pool. "I think that's enough talk about such matters. Grandpa's poor heart can't handle it. Wait here."

Bernie went through the large glass doors and fished a wrapped present out from one of the drawers in the living room. He returned to see Nova staring far off across the L.A. hills, the ice cream melting in his hand. Bernie took his seat by his grandson, hiding the present, and rang a small bell.

"Grandpa, are you rich?" Nova asked, staring out into the L.A. horizon.

"Why would you ask that?" Bernie replied, mildly embarrassed.

"Some kids at school said I couldn't go to Reecey's birthday because my grandpa is rich."

Bernie sighed.

"I'm going to be honest with you, okay? Yes, I have a lot of money, but no one gave it to me, and I sacrificed my health and relationships for it." Nova listened closely. "Sometimes Grandpa gets sick, you know why?"

Nova shook his head, "no."

"Well, because I'm rich."

Bernie continued, "But if those kids make fun of you again, tell them, yes, your grandpa is rich, and you are too."

"I'm rich too?" Nova responded excitedly.

"Yes, do you know how I know?"

"No..."

"Because your legs and arms work, your smile works, your mind works, you're a good boy and you know where you come from, and you treat people the way you want to be treated. Is that true?"

Nova nodded yes with confidence.

"So, actually, you are super rich!" Bernie pointed to his grandson's heart.

"Super?" Nova's eyes lit up.

"Super-duper-ooper rich. And if you're lucky, these qualities will help you get a lot of money too."

Nova laughed and spilled his ice cream.

"Lennox, would you fetch a wet towel for Nova here, something to clean up his hands?" Bernie said without a glance in the butler's direction.

"Right away, sir."

Nova's mind quickly remembered the kidnapping.

"I don't want to get kidnapped," he finally said.

"Now, now." Bernie reached an arm around Nova. "Don't you worry one little hair on your head. Nothing like that will happen to you. Look how protected you are." Bernie gestured around the mansion.

"No harm will come to you. I promise. Now, here..." A moment later, Lennox appeared in the opening of the glass doors and delivered a pile of napkins. Bernie took it from the butler without a word. "Wash your hands and clean yourself off. I have something for you."

Nova began to follow Bernie. Bernie stopped and bent down and whispered to Nova.

"Go say thank you to Lennox for the napkins. They work for me, but they don't have to."

Nova did as he was asked. He always did what grandpa asked.

"Thank you, Lennox."

"You're most welcome, sir," Lennox responded before disappearing into the mansion.

"Popsi..." Nova pulled at his grandfather's pants.

"Yes, son?"

"Is Lennox different?"

"Yes."

"Why is Lennox different?"

"Can I ask you a question?"

"Yah." Nova giggled.

"If I told you to stay awake for five days, could you do it?"

"No! I would be sleepy."

"Can you control it?"

"No, because my body would go to sleep."

"Ah ha! So you can't control it?"

"No."

"Should people be mean to you because you can't stay awake for five days?"

"No! That's not nice. It's not my fault."

"Lennox is different from you, and it's not their fault."

"Do you understand?"

Nova nodded.

"How does Lennox make you feel?"

"Good, he always helps me and takes care of me. I think he's part of our family."

"Son, one more thing—Lennox asked me not to call them 'he.'

Nova interjected. "But..."

"Should we be mean to people who are different and can't control it?"

"No."

"Good. Lennox told me the word 'he' makes them feel uncomfortable. At first I didn't understand, but it's not kind to make family feel uncomfortable, is it?"

"No."

"Life is complex, son. I'll tell you more when you get older, okay?"

Nova smiled and cheerfully agreed as Bernie patted his head. "Good boy."

Bernie grinned and placed the wrapped object on the table. Nova eagerly reached for it, but Bernie put a hand over his before he could take it. "Before you open it, I want you to know that it is very expensive, and you are to take the utmost care with it. Is that understood?"

Nova nodded with excited eyes.

"That's a good boy." Bernie took his hand away. "Go ahead," he gestured with a smile.

Nova carefully opened the wrapping. He wasn't like other boys his age who would simply rip into it like they were tearing at flesh. Instead, Nova unfolded each corner of tape and unraveled it with delicate precision. Nova knew his grandfather expected him to control his excitement.

It was a book.

Nova read the title out loud: *The Hound of the Baskervilles.*

"I know how much you enjoy your reading, so this is something for you to read. Have you ever heard of Sherlock Holmes?"

Nova shook his head.

"Oh, then you are in for a treat. Once you read it, your life will never be the same. This book very much inspired who I am today."

Nova was already flipping through the pages as Bernie spoke. "Look on the publication page." The old man continued, showing Nova the publication details. "It's a first edition. Not many of those are left around in such good condition. It will be worth quite a fortune someday."

"Thank you, Popsi!" Nova hopped out of his seat and hugged Bernie with the intimacy only the innocence of childhood can inspire.

"Oh, no." Bernie chuckled. "Careful now; you'll crush Grandpa in that strong grip of yours." Nova laughed and plopped himself back on his chair, carefully leafing through the first pages. Bernie beamed as he watched the serious concentration on his grandson's face.

"One day, Nova, you will follow in my footsteps. I just wish I could be around to see it. I tried with your father, but..."

But Nova wasn't listening. Nor would he remember the words his grandfather spoke when the old man left everything to him in his will over a decade later. However, he would remember how his grandfather made him feel, the tangible and intangible gifts of safety and trust left behind, and his duty to continue the Crenshaw legacy.

Ten years ago

The day wound into night, and eleven-year-old Nova found himself staring up at the faraway ceiling of his room in Grandpa's mansion. He had spent hours trying to read, scanning the images of mystery and murder, and the great deductive mind of Holmes raced through his head. Nova thought he wanted to be just like Holmes. Not only because the detective was a genius, but because, to Nova, the fictional man was a projection of his Popsi, Grandpa Bernie.

Nova had unconsciously equated the one with the other. Sometimes, Nova wandered into his grandpa's study and found all sorts of mathematical equations and blueprints. To him, Bernie was as close to magic as magic gets. And he yearned to follow in his grandpa's footsteps.

It took a long while for his thoughts to stop whirring and before his body fell into sleep, and when it did, he dreamed.

He found himself walking down a long corridor. It was dark and full of cobwebs, barely lit by the flicker of torches on the wall. At the end of the hallway was a staircase that descended into shadows. Nova had never liked the dark, but he was dressed in detective clothes and knew that this was no time for fear. He took a torch from the wall and began the slow creep downwards. Every step creaked into the whispers of witches, guised in the phantom words of Holmes and Watson. Back in his bed, Nova's eyes were darting back and forth beneath his eyelids.

He wound round and round, deep into the underbelly of darkness, until finally, his foot stepped onto a bedrock of concrete. He couldn't make anything out around him, so he took another step forward. As he did, Nova felt something soft beneath his foot. Hoping he had not just stepped on a mouse, he lifted his shoe with one eye closed. The instant he saw what was beneath his foot, his heart leaped from his chest. A sensation of free-falling ensued, descending for what felt like miles and miles. His pulse drummed wildly as the light from the torch revealed striped suspenders.

Nova gasped and dropped the torch, submerging him into darkness again. In one burst, he woke back into his body and tried to scream. But, as he tried, no sound came out of his mouth. He tried to move, but his body was frozen. Only his eyes were free of the paralysis that locked his consciousness in sleeping skin, frantically darting as he hollered bloody murder in his mind. From beneath the crack of the door, a shadow rose. Nova struggled to break free from the spell of being bound. He was powerless, and the shadow was drawing nearer. Yellow eyes glowed within the dark fur, and a low grumbling snarl filled the room.

Just as the shadow's claws were about to touch Nova's skin, he awoke. His holler tore through the silent fabric of the mansion. And when Bernie finally entered Nova's room, the young boy was huddled in the corner of his bed with his knees hugged close to his chest, rocking. Bernie rushed to Nova's side, as fast as a man in his seventies could go, and coddled his terrified grandson in his arms.

"Shh. Everything's all right. Shh. It was just a bad dream."

But, as much as Grandpa Bernie tried to soothe him, Nova couldn't forget the striped suspenders in the shadows of that empty basement and the glare of yellow eyes getting ever closer in the freeze of nightmares. And so it was for many years.

After a while, age and time pushed the memory of the nightmare away. And soon, as most children do, Nova forgot what happened that night.

But like all shadows that linger in the past, they have a way of returning. Returning when we least expect it, and so too would this memory return, a long time ahead, when the shadows were long gone, and when he was at last ready to face an unimaginable reality about his ancestors.

* * *

"I can't fucking believe this!" Nova heard his father Eric's shouts echoing through the house. The sound of slamming doors began shortly after. Shattered glass and broken furniture littered the ground. Nova sat on the edge of his bed with his eyes staring blankly at the floor by his feet.

"Don't give me that shit. I'm his fucking son, Stella! His son! Unbelievable."

Nova tuned out the sounds of his father screaming. It had become a skill of his, one he had learned early in life. The world drowned away, and his vision blurred around the edges when Eric drank and screamed. A numb cocoon enveloped Nova, and he looked up to the light hanging from his ceiling, it being his only focus. His father's screams became muted thuds against a high-pitched ringing in his soundscape. Nova squinted his eyes, and the light transformed into long stretching rays, carrying him into another world of sparkling flakes and strings of light.

Eric tore down the long-draped curtains that hung on the window across from his bed.

"Stop!" Stella shouted, a hand over her face as she turned away from her rampaging husband.

Eric's head snapped in her direction. A cold, deadly stare washed over his face, and the anger practically rumbled off him. "Don't. You. Dare."

He pointed an accusing finger in her face. A second later, he had her cheeks in his grip, squeezing her face as tears streamed from her bloodshot eyes. "Don't you say another fucking word."

He released her with a push, and Nova's mother crumpled to the ground. Even though tears streamed down her face involuntarily, her expression was hard. She had taken this abuse many times. She was used to it now. All she had to do was comply and wait until Eric left, which he always did. Eric grabbed keys from a small desk in their room and slipped on his suit jacket. Stella looked up at him, hating herself more for crying than the hate she felt for Eric.

"Where are you going?" she asked coldly. "I, I..."

"To the fucking lawyer. I'm getting that money whether that old dirtbag likes it or not. How could he let his only son suffer?"

From the blurred corner of Nova's vision, he saw the movement of his father leaving. The sound of Eric's footsteps made its way through Nova's dissociated ears. He turned and numbly watched his father speed off. Only when his father was gone did Nova feel the heat of his own anger rise. He pulled off his shoe and threw it at the wall. He knew he was the only one who could save his mother. But was he strong enough? Was it his responsibility to save her? Should he tell Grandpa Bernie? Adults save themselves, but Stella was not strong enough yet to save herself. The shoe tumbled lamely to the ground. The quick-rising anger dissipated for what lay at the core of his feelings. Grief. Grieving someone who was alive and sensing a relationship he never had slip further away. Seeing his father's face yet looking into the eyes of a stranger. Nova buried his face into his pillow and yelled his cries out into the place where no one would hear them.

CHAPTER THREE

Through the Looking Glass

Present day

"Holy shit... My face is melting!" Magenta moaned in ecstasy as the music blared on max volume in fast-paced twists and curves of sound.

She was twirling her fingers in the air, lying upside-down on the couch. The pattern she wove in rhythm to the music left traces of rainbow silk like her arms were moving frame by frame through time. The stars were bright in the sky, clear through the glass skylight above. The lighting was low. The room was lit by a bisexually colored pink, purple, and blue lava lamp that Magenta had brought. It resembled a cloud, and Nova was transfixed on it as it pulsed from soft blues to bright purple, pink, and red.

Pearl danced like a mermaid, moving slowly and fluidly like a sway of seaweed from side to side. Nova was drawn to the light curves of her hips as he suppressed his shame for being interested in his friend. Her eyes were closed, and she seemed to be in a world of her own. Ruben emerged from the pool against the light of the moon. Every inch of his body defined in tattoos and glistening muscles.

"Ruben!" Magenta called out with a dazed smile.

He strode over to her, drying himself off with a towel, and sat against the couch beside her. Her fingers came to trace the strong chisel line of his jaw. Magenta was still upside down as their foreheads came to press against one another. Their eyes met, and the silence was filled with a thousand unspoken words. Ruben leaned in, and Magenta closed the remaining distance, the soft of her full lips meeting his. Their tongues twined like song light. Ruben and Magenta had crossed the line from friendship to lovers several months back and had been unsure how to tell Nova and Pearl that they had become friends but with benefits and benefits that made money on OnlyFans.

"Holy shit," Ruben said, drawing back, his lips wet with the taste of her. "This is the cleanest shit I've ever had."

Magenta let out a witchy laugh before pulling him back in toward her. Nova was smiling like crazy as he watched them, and Pearl came to plop on the cushion beside him.

"About time," Pearl whispered.

"I know. They've been dancing around one another for months. Although I doubt this is their first time. They think we're stupid."

"I'm pretty sure I saw them hooking up last week." Pearl smirked. "But it's just like them to keep it unofficial. I think they enjoy 'the game' way too much."

Magenta pulled away from Ruben and swung her legs around the couch, standing up and swaying over to her rainbow chrome bag. She paused as she crouched down, getting lost for a moment in the trance-inducing light waves and patterns that swirled over its shimmering surface.

"What was I doing again?" she muttered to herself.

Then her memory kicked in to remind her, and she laughed at herself for how high she was. She unzipped the bag and pulled out a rectangular object wrapped in a colorful Indian patterned cloth.

"What have you got there?" Ruben asked as Magenta waltzed back over to the couch as graceful as a cat.

Magenta wiggled her eyebrows at him playfully before sitting down and laying the cloth on the table. She captivated everyone's attention as she slowly unwrapped the colorful folds of fabric.

Nova frowned when he saw what was inside. "A deck of cards? I'm sorry, but I don't think I have the wits to play."

"I second that," Pearl added.

"Oh, this isn't just any deck of cards." Magenta said mysteriously, meeting everyone's eyes one by one. "This is a tarot deck."

She put her hand on top of the deck and swirled out the cards, so they were still all face down but arranged in a circle.

"Ooh cool!" Pearl exclaimed. "I got a tarot reading once from a guy who called himself Rabbit."

Ruben turned to Pearl in disbelief.

"Pearl, sorry to break it to you, but Rabbit is a pimp. Everyone knows that!"

Pearl scowled.

Nova peered at Pearl with a smirk. "And you would trust someone who calls themselves Rabbit?"

Pearl raised her hands defensively. "I did it for fun. My friend convinced me to do it. And I've got to say; it was freaky. The guy looked into my eyes, and I swear he was reading my mind. It was quite creepy, actually. He started telling me things about myself that he could never have known."

"Umm...did you ever think he could have Googled you?" Nova asked sarcastically.

"All right, everyone, settle down." Magenta said, gaining control of the room again. "Nova, just keep an open mind, okay?" She added, giving him a little wink. "Tarot works in ways that are hard for the conscious mind to understand. I'm going to start selling readings next month."

Her fingers hovered over the circle of face-down cards as if scanning for something. Nova watched and found himself being drawn into the process. There was a mystical tension in the room, and everyone was on the edge of their seat. Magenta moved over a card and then suddenly doubled back on herself. She pulled it free from the rest and flipped it over.

She smiled as she set it down for all to see. The tension defused as they saw what was illustrated on the front of the card. There was a deific, angel-looking being in the sky with its hands outstretched, and below it was a man and a woman standing naked next to two fruit trees. The tree beside the female had a snake coiled around it, and at the bottom of the card were two words: "The Lovers."

"No fucking way," Ruben said from beside Magenta.

Nova laughed at the synchronicity of the draw.

"This one speaks for itself," Magenta said coolly. "Perfect partnership, desires, temptation..." She looked over to Nova and Pearl. "And a newly kindled romantic interest."

Nova blushed. He and Pearl exchanged a look with one another, and he felt a strong pull to her in his heart. Maybe there was something to these cards after all.

"Now, we can't only pull one," Magenta continued. "Tarot is most powerful when multiple cards are pulled because together, they tell a story. Let us see what tonight has in store for us, shall we?"

41

She drew another. "Hmm. The High Priestess. A very powerful card. One of mystery. The High Priestess only appears when a woman of exceptional power is nearby; she is the great revealer, the card that whispers great knowledge, unveiling truths that spark a time of great decision-making. Things are not what they seem, and it will do everyone well to trust your inner instincts when presented with a challenging situation."

Nova frowned. He wasn't sure what to make of that one, but there wasn't much time to ponder it because Magenta was already pulling another card.

"The Knight of Swords. One of you may be called to action, forced to fight for that closest to your heart. The Knight of Swords is always in action and never still. His sword is raised and ready for battle, whatever the challenge may be."

"Judgment," Magenta said through narrow eyes as she pulled the next card. "The card of resurrection and decision-making. Something in one of our lives is coming to an end. The horns of judgment call down for one of us to step into a new role."

"And finally," Magenta pulled the last card.

Everyone was on the edge of their seats. Nova felt like he did when he was a kid, back when his grandfather used to read him stories at night.

"Oh..." Magenta's voice trailed off, and her face appeared a little disturbed.

"What is it?" Pearl said.

Magenta bit her lip and slowly placed the card down on the table for everyone to see. Nova felt a stab of fear as he looked at the card. There was a pitch-black background with a large tower standing on sharp rocks. Lightning struck the tower, and flames flared from the windows. Two people were falling, plummeting to their deaths on the rocks below.

"What does it mean?" Nova found himself saying.

"Umm. There are many possible interpretations," Magenta said vaguely. But she could not hide her expression of worry as she stared at the card.

Ruben cleared his throat. "Boring! What a load of shit. Everyone, get over here!"

He lifted Magenta up and grabbed her ass, earning a delightful yelp. In a single instant, the entire atmosphere in the room changed, and Nova laughed as he watched Magenta playfully try to wriggle out of Ruben's grasp. The cards were forgotten in an instant, thanks to the short memory attributed to the great flow of LSD in their blood.

Ruben buried his face in Magenta's chest and began to kiss his way up to her neck.

"Oh my God!" Pearl shielded her eyes jokingly and exchanged a grossed-out look with Nova.

Ruben growled and l up from Magenta's neck. "Pearl, Nova. Get over here."

Magenta laughed and turned herself around.

"No thanks, I don't wanna make out with you, bro," Nova teased back. "Unless you want me to throw up in your mouth." He shrugged.

"Aww, come on. We can record it and put it on my OnlyFans."

"That's so hot–I love gay porn," Magenta said.

Pearl shook her head, laughing, "I'm not mature enough for this."

"I love when a little tiny twink..." Magenta pretended to break a stick, "Pop!" she said. Ruben exploded in laughter.

Pearl fished a clove cigarette from the open pack on the table, putting her feet up over Nova's lap. "Unlike you, I'd prefer to keep my sex life *off* the internet." She lit the cigarette and took a deep inhale. The smoke appeared blue in the light of the cloud lamp. "I have no beef with sex workers, but, like, what if I became famous by accident and everyone could see my pussy? Like, where's your credibility if the world has seen your pussy?"

"No risk, no reward," Ruben joked.

"Nov, we gotta get you laid, though. I don't understand how you're still a virgin."

"I'm happy being a virgin. I'll have sex when I'm ready," Nova said. Pearl gazed over at him and smiled with admiration.

"Nova, I love you, bro, but I read a statistic that said just one percent of 18 to 34-year-olds are virgins. So, I guess my best bud is the one percent." Ruben high-fived Nova.

"Would someone who makes money by showing their ass on camera understand virginity?" Pearl said sarcastically.

"Idea!" Ruben responded.

"Do you know how many viewers we'd get if Nova *lost* his virginity on camera?"

"New subject, please. I feel sick," Pearl said, motioning Magenta to control Ruben. Nova watched calmly.

Magenta took her place behind Ruben and gave him a sensual head scratch with her claw-like fingernails. Ruben's eyes rolled to the back of his head as tingles were sent shivering over his body. "Well, I'm shooting some content this weekend."

"Hell, fuck it. I'm down." Magenta shrugged with a look of pure mischief in her eyes.

"Magenta!" Pearl exclaimed.

"What?! I don't show my face. Throw me my purse. I brought something." She gestured with her hands.

Pearl was in amused disbelief as she threw the faux leather purse over.

"Thank you, my love." Magenta winked and took her hands off Ruben's head.

"No. Don't stop."

"Hold up." Magenta smiled, reaching into her purse and pulling out a lavender mask like they used to wear in old masquerades.

"Yes!" Ruben exclaimed. "That's hot. Come here."

He pulled her in again, and Magenta moaned as he rose and pressed himself into her barely clothed body.

Pearl sighed. "Want to take a walk? This is our exit."

Nova was relieved. "Yes, please!"

Pearl jumped up and took his hand, and they made off for the back door.

"Suit yourselves!" Ruben called out after them as he set up his camera equipment.

But they were already out of the living room and passing through the long corridor that led to the part of the mansion overlooking the woods.

"Mmm. The fresh air feels good," Pearl whispered, twirling around like a woodland fairy.

Nova watched her in silent yearning. The insects were chirping in the mountain trees all around them, and they seemed to sing Pearl into motion. She paused and noticed Nova's gaze, blushing slightly and biting her lower lip. With a flirty gesture, she offered the clove cigarette to him in an outstretched hand.

"Thanks," Nova whispered, taking it from her. "Where are we walking?"

"I don't know," Pearl said with a smile, the drugs working their magic on her. "It just feels good to move. And the ground feels amazing against my feet." She giggled. "Sorry. I'm high...I feel like I'm watching us from above."

"My grandpa has a cabin back here. Maybe we can walk there?"

"Oh, my God. Perfect."

Nova was never really the one to make the first move, but Pearl was glowing, and he couldn't hold himself back from perceiving signals from her. Most days, Nova's hormones screamed and hollered for him to act, but he never learned how. He never saw his parents kiss or being overtly romantic, and his grandfather was very conservative about topics of sex. But something about Pearl made him feel safe. He could envision his first experience being with her.

Nova reached out his hand lightly and took hers. A wave of warm electricity washed through both as their skin made contact. Nova dropped the clove cigarette on the ground, and he pulled her, gently as a feather, toward him. Her chest touched his, and energy coursed through him. He could feel Pearl's heart beating; they were breathing the same air. He bent down to kiss her, and their lips met for a fraction of a second before a loud crack startled them from their intimate moment.

Pearl peeled away, her head snapping in the direction of the sound. "Magenta?"

Nova sighed.

There was no answer. Only the sound of crickets and nighttime insects responded.

"Ruben, if that's you..." Still silent. She turned to Nova. "You heard that, right? I'm not just trippin'?"

Nova shrugged, disappointed that his moment had been cut short. "It was probably an animal or something. Maybe we're being stalked by a mountain lion."

Pearl nudged him and froze in fear. "If that was a mountain lion, it must be high too, tripping on twigs like that."

She linked her arm in his and looked around one last time before they continued on deeper into the trees. Pearl tried to conceal her panic from Nova, but the forest sounds triggered her paranoia.

"So, he has a cabin back here?" Pearl asked.

"Yes, it's not far. He used it for a lot of his research stuff before he retired."

"What did he do? I never asked you."

"He was a geneticist. Research and genetic mapping kinda stuff."

"Oh, yeah! That's right!" Pearl continued.

The two talked softly with one another, both still tender after the brief touch of intimacy. Nova listened with all his attention as Pearl unfurled parts of her heart and story, chiming in at the right moments, which was always met with a smile from her. They created a bubble of their own world, discussing their family and hopes for adulthood. Time became a thing of distant memory, and they were so entranced with one another's voices and presence that they didn't notice the shift of sound in the air. They didn't notice the insect's voices growing further away or the dead rustle of leaves that hung silent like a coiled snake waiting to strike.

Nova was deep in a flow of outspoken thought when Pearl froze on his arm. "Nova," she said, interrupting him mid-sentence. Her voice was tense like metal in the air.

Nova frowned. When he looked at her, there was genuine fear on her face. At first, he smirked. "What's wrong?"

"Shh!" she whispered. "There's someone there."

"The cabin is the only thing up this high. It's probably an animal..."

He turned to see where her eyes were locked and shook his head, not seeing anything. "There's nothing there."

He was about to make a joke when he felt a hot breeze against his right cheek. Frowning, he turned. Every cell in his body recoiled. "Holy fuck!"

Pearl screamed, and her nails dug into Nova's arm.

Standing a few meters away was a corpse of a white man. He stood dead still against the light of the moon, facing their direction. His eyes had been removed, and in their place were deep, dark sockets carved into his skull, severed nerve endings, and exposed blood vessels. And, like roots emerging from the darkness, razor-thin cuts branched out every which way against his skin.

Nova and Pearl were frozen. If Ruben had been there, he might have yelled at them to run, or he would have charged right at the eyeless man without a second thought. They say you never know your instinct until it's put to the test, and Nova and Pearl were paralyzed with surprise.

The man held out cupped hands at the height of his waist. He didn't move. He stood there.

Pearl was the first to break out of the freeze. She pulled Nova back against the bark of a tree, not letting her eyes leave the hollow man's shape. "Nova," she whispered in an urgent tone. He was trying to reply, but his mind kept going into shock and disbelief like a record stuck on scratch. "Nova!" she said again, this time physically shaking him and forcing him back into reality. She giggled, muttering, "It's the weed, right, or?" Nova came to and grabbed Pearl's hand. His eyes were wide and full of confusion.

"I see it too."

"It's staring at us."

"Nova, we need to fucking go."

He nodded, shaking slightly. This all felt so familiar. Like he was living it again, in some fucked up déjà vu.

They both looked at one another and then back to the man. It was only then that he launched toward them.

This time they ran.

"Which way is the house!" Pearl yelled.

"I have no fucking idea!"

Pearl's soft feet scratched against the rough ground. She stubbed her toe against an exposed root, but Nova was there to catch her before she could fall. She ignored the pain and kept running with a limp, for the sound of footsteps that weren't their own was grinding behind.

"Fuck! It's chasing us, Nova!"

Terror began to sprout from the soil in physical form. Mangled hands broke through the ground, scraping madly to break free. Between the trees, ghoulish faces appeared with dislocated jaws and dribbling spit, all moaning and reaching toward Pearl and Nova.

"What the fuck is in this acid!" Pearl yelled.

Nova let the possibility of a bad trip play out; it was the only thing keeping him sane. That this was all some sort of strange hallucination, and the effects would wear off in an hour or two.

But, for some reason, he knew that whatever was happening was not due to the psychedelics.

Pearl was in a terror frenzy of her own. Running for her life like a bunny fleeing from serpentine jaws. The disembodied hands and arms climbed through the soil, reaching for their ankles. Nova felt them grabbing at his foot as he kicked them away.

"Ruben!" Nova screamed, finally finding his voice again. "Help! Ruben! Magenta!"

There was no reply, but he could hear the faint sound of electronic music in the distance. They ran in the direction of the upbeat tempo. The footsteps and rustling leaves kept getting louder. Pearl was fighting tears as she ran through the pain, leaving a breadcrumb trail of blood from her scratched foot. They could make out the lights from the mansion in the distance.

"There it is!" Pearl yelled.

They were about to reach the border of the land plot, where the gate and walls stood tall like barricades, when something large crashed into them. This was it. It had caught them.

CHAPTER FOUR

Black Pawn

Forty-five years ago

Eric had managed to slip out of bed and past Lennox's quarters unheard. Under his arm, he carried a carved wooden chess set. He had gotten it for his seventh birthday last week, which he had spent alone with Lennox in front of the television.

Bernie had been away speaking at the 'World Changer' conference in Seattle, one of the largest media events in the county to celebrate black people making a difference in their respective industries. Bernie had won an award for excellence in biological sciences, specifically genetic sequencing research. Eric was awestruck that his father was the same man spotlighted in news articles and photographed with Jimmy Carter and famous celebrities.

Eric had watched his father on television while opening his Christmas presents, all picked out by Lennox with 'From Dad' forged on the tags. He could identify his father's writing and signature within a fraction of a second, but still, he accepted these gifts with the tags written by Lennox.

"Look what Daddy got me," Eric said to his mother, Madeline, who was busy laughing on the phone.

Madeline shut the door.

Eric stood disappointed and motionless.

One night, the light in Bernie's study was still on, and light seeped in from under the crack of the door into the dark hallway. Eric was a small boy and only had to bend slightly to peer in through the keyhole. Eric frowned. He could only see black. Suddenly, the door swung open, and Eric nearly fell into the study. He looked up to see his father, Bernie, standing over him, his face darkened as the light from the study draped over his shoulders.

"What are you doing here?"

Eric cowered away under the towering presence of his father, partly amazed, partly terrified. He was a soft-spoken boy, and as he replied, "Do you want to play..." Bernie interrupted him.

"Stop mumbling when you speak. Stand up straight. Chest out. Don't be a sissy."

Eric forwent speaking for fear of further chastisement and instead held up the chessboard for his father to see with the large eyes and soft heart of a whimpering animal.

Bernie spared it a passing glance. "What is this?"

Eric responded joyfully, "The chess set you got me."

Bernie looked briefly confused before responding, "Do I look like I have time to play games? Do you eat if I play games?"

Bernie brushed past Eric, leaving him standing alone in his cow-print pajamas in the doorway with his chessboard.

"Lennox!" Bernie called down the stairs. "Take Eric and Madeline around for dinner and shopping. I'll be working late in my cabin." Bernie pulled out several hundred-dollar bills from his vintage leather wallet. "And play a round of chess with the boy. He should be playing very well by now." Bernie poured himself a glass of Bourbon.

"Lennox! Do you hear me?" Bernie mumbled in frustration. *Do I pay you to ignore me?*

Lennox rushed up the stairs and took Eric by the hand, pulling him toward the bedroom. As Lennox pulled him, Eric lost his grip on the chess set. He reached for the board with his small, outstretched hand, but Lennox continued to tug him away.

The wooden pieces scattered to the edges of the floor, except for a single black pawn that tumbled into the light and landed upright. Eric let Lennox drag him, but his eyes never left the single black pawn. His eyes transfixed as if spellbound to a part of himself that he would never see again and his position in Bernie's mind as unworthy of time.

* * *

Over the years, Eric grew used to Bernie's absence, and in the aftermath of his mother Madeline's death, he took out his unconscious anger and loneliness on things smaller than himself. He often brought his magnifying lens into the heat of the L.A. hills and set the focal lens to the sun, preying on small anthills and watching their tiny insect bodies roast.

One time, while poking around on a small hill, Eric found a toad hole. He forced the toad out with the long edge of a stick and, for reasons unknown, squashed it under the weight of a heavy rock. When he lifted the rock, he discovered that the organs of the victimized amphibian had burst into a pool of guts and blood. He stared at the guts expressionlessly, aware of what he had done but without remorse. As Eric grew, he took on larger animals, shooting down squirrels and birds with a slingshot he had made himself.

He could take to his hobbies in peace, as his father was never at home while busy becoming famous, renowned, and loved by strangers, and Lennox only had so much influence over him. By the time Eric was a teenager, even Lennox had no sway over him, and he soon took to killing animals with Bernie's rifles.

Lennox had observed Eric becoming more violent and instinctively knew the accumulated trauma of Bernie's absence and his mother's death had impacted him in profound ways, yet Lennox found it most appropriate to neither speak nor become involved in the family's personal matters.

Eric's deeds went unnoticed until he took his first weapon to school.

* * *

Bernie and Eric rushed out of the *L.A. Times* newspaper building into the extended cab Mercedes as overcast clouds began to fill the sky. Eric sat looking out of the window in the backseat of the car, pockmarks of adolescence fresh and pustulant on his face. Eric was eager to join his father in publicity events but resented his father and his supporters. Eric often wondered *if these people only knew his father the way he knew him,* they would not be so eager to celebrate him. The tension in the car was thick and drawn tight.

"Lennox, call ahead to this restaurant and make sure I won't be sitting on any synthetic fabrics."

"Yes, sir."

"Can you believe that the receptionist asked me if I was applying to be a building janitor?"

Lennox nodded his head.

"Should I call the executive editor to have her fired?" Bernie looked over at Eric with a stern face. "You gonna let people call your father a janitor, boy?"

Lennox laughed in response.

"And she was so genuine about it. I should have asked her, 'Hunny, do you realize my suit costs more than your salary? Racist bitch.'"

Lennox did not respond.

"One day, I'm an award-winning geneticist, the next moment, I'm cleaning toilets," Bernie scoffed. "Sounds like America..."

Bernie had given his son no verbal chastisement, but the thick silence did more than any words could. Eric wished his dad would yell and admonish him. At least that would show he knew his son was alive. Lennox drove smoothly through the winding Hollywood hills, glancing every now and then to the back seat through the rearview mirror.

Bernie broke the silence. "I'm sending you away." Eric didn't bother to look away from the window. In his mind, he felt he had never existed.

"The Oakland Military Institute in the Bay Area," Bernie fished out a booklet from a leather folder and placed it on the middle seat. "And...you leave tomorrow."

Eric felt nothing as his father spoke. A numbness, which was, in fact, anger that seethed and bubbled under the surface but had no will to burst. Numbness was all Eric felt these days, coupled with an agonizing rage without the sweet pleasure of release.

"The rifle, the squirrels, the burning of animals...did you forget we have security cameras?" Bernie continued flipping through his folder. "I've done all I can do. And those poor animals that had the misfortune of meeting you."

"You need discipline," he added. "Structure. And a reminder of the real world. My money doesn't mean it's your money. And my money doesn't make you white. You can't just pussyfoot around. This is a heartless, racist game. And you're soft. I've done what I can to..."

"You've done nothing!" Rage exploded through Eric like an awakened volcano.

"Lennox, stop the car." Lennox pulled the car over to the curb and rolled up the privacy window.

Eric ranted out a monologue for several minutes. Bernie listened to Eric calmly, having already made his decision.

"Mom is dead! She's dead. You've said nothing. Have you even noticed? Did you even love her?" Eric shouted, unable to control his tears. "You're like...a sociopath."

Bernie pointed his finger in his son's face. "Watch your mouth. You will not speak about my wife in that way. Love is all I do. And I get *nothing* back for it."

"Your wife?" Eric laughed. "Your wife who you cheated on and had some secret daughter no one knows about? Well, she knew, and I know. You're pathetic, Bernard."

Bernie hit Eric across the face with a closed fist.

Silence encapsulated the car as rain hit the windows.

Bernie regained his composure to quickly conceal his moment of fury. "Please exit my car. Lennox will prepare a bag and leave it outside the gate."

"Whatever, Bernard. Fuck off." Eric slammed the car door and ran into the darkness.

Bernie sat still for several seconds, outraged that Eric had broken his self-control. Bernie felt that he had done everything for his son. Sent him to the best schools, ensured he had everything he wanted and more, yet he could not understand how Eric could instinctively reject his effort to provide. Bernie felt guilty that his son had been spoiled by unrelatable privilege and freedom. Eric was, in fact, ignorant to the real struggles of the world, a world which, for Bernie, was filled with people doubting his every move. A world where people interpreted his presence as offensive. A world without trust. If only Eric knew the scope of the sacrifices Bernie had made. Every moment Bernie was alive was spent securing the Crenshaw legacy, but it was becoming clear that Eric did not have what it took to follow in his footsteps. Eric was seduced by emotion and ran from logic. It was too late for his son now. The damages, the seen and unseen wounds, were irreparable.

* * *

Nova was four when his grandfather retired. Eric was away on a business trip, and Stella had taken Nova to Bernie's house for the first time. He remembered the look of shock when Bernie saw his mother and then awe as Bernie's eyes passed over to him. Like a cool breeze had hit Bernie's face. Stella and Bernie talked in whispers that Nova couldn't hear, but his attention was on other things. Primarily the June bugs buzzing in the long grass outside the house.

"I am going to leave you with your Grandpa Bernie, Nova," his mother said softly.

"Be good, and I'll be back to pick you up later tonight."

Stella gave her son a hug, and he watched her get in the car and drive off.

A hand came to rest on his shoulder, and he looked up to see the old man his mother had said was his grandpa. Bernie kneeled and smiled. Nova was drawn to the love in his eyes like a moth to a flame. Nova touched Bernie's eyelid to point out that his eyes were different colors.

"Yes, son. One brown, one green, just like you." Bernie understood the silent language of his grandson.

"You and I are going to have a lot of fun today." Bernie took Nova's hand. "Now, your mother tells me you like books. We have a lot of those here. A whole library, in fact."

Hand in hand, Bernie guided his grandson into the mansion, and for the first time, he felt hopeful about the future of the Crenshaw family.

One year after Bernie's death

Eric came home drunk. Nova had been asleep when he awoke to the tumble of something close by. Eric sat in a chair across from the bed, his silhouette outlined in the sliver of moonlight shining through Nova's bedroom window, a bottle of liquor in his right hand. Nova sat up suddenly in bed, and for a long moment, the father and son shared an exchange of silence, emotions ringing in the air across taut and unspoken threads.

"You ungrateful little shit," Eric scoffed and put the bottle to his lips, taking a large swing. Nova could smell the rank of spirit and sweat so strongly it burned his nostrils. Still, Nova didn't dare speak.

"He didn't do this for you, you know," Eric continued. His voice was rough and scratchy, dulled, and impaired by liquor and cigarettes. "He's never loved anyone but his work and whatever the fuck he's been building in that cabin. He is a soulless creature." Another swig. "He just did this to spite me."

Nova felt his chest tighten as if a large metal weight had just been hung from a chain on his sternum.

"He couldn't face what he did to me. I know everything," Eric scoffed drunkenly again. "All he gave to you was not out of love; it was out of guilt. You're a guilty side thought. Something to help him sleep at night."

Nova glared at his father, now threatened by criticism of Bernie.

"Well? You gonna say anything?"

Nova clenched his jaw to hold in words he knew would provoke his father. Eric scoffed again. "How I raised such a pussy, I'll never know."

He threw the empty bottle to the floor, and it clunked hard against the wood, the glass too thick to shatter, then slid to the base of Nova's bed.

"You didn't raise me!" Nova snapped, fire overtaking his limbs. Before he even knew it, he was across the room and pinning his father to the wall, an arm to Eric's throat. "You haven't done shit for me. Drunk piece of shit. I fucking hate you!"

Nova's fury flared in his father's face, but even pinned against the wall, Eric didn't flinch. His eyes were still dead from the dullness brought by the drink. And after a moment, Eric began to laugh. Nova frowned, confused by the snicker snaking out of his father, and backed away. His father slid down the wall, his laughter rising into hysterical chokes as the pressure from Nova's arm against his throat was released.

"What the hell are you laughing at?!" Nova yelled, looking down on his father.

"This is Bernie, can't you see? Look what he's done to you." Eric broke into laughter again. Although Eric was an addict, he knew Nova's disposition. And Nova was not oriented toward violence.

Nova scowled and shook his head. "You and I are nothing alike."

"But we are!" Eric continued. "The longer you lie to yourself, the more like me you become. You think I haven't heard those words before?" Eric stumbled to his feet, taking several seconds to find his balance.

Suddenly Eric had his palm behind Nova's head, pulling his son in close so that both their foreheads were touching. "I lived those words. I once loved Bernard too. But I won't send you away. That's love." Eric wobbled in place. "I won't send you away to get fucking molested in a dorm room."

Nova looked at his father, concerned.

"Yeah, Grandpa Bernie sent your dad away to get bullied and molested. Do you even care?"

"Me and you...we're in this," Eric continued.

The reek of Eric's breath hung rancid in the air as Nova pulled himself free from his father's grip. "I know you wish Mister Bernie, or what did you call him"-Eric made quotation gestures with his fingers-"*Popsi* was your father instead of me, but the old bastard is a piece of shit, I promise."

Eric continued, "I know I'm not the best, okay? but I respect you enough not to lie to your fucking face." He swayed a little on his feet. "Bernie was off. Lennox too."

Nova narrowed his eyes in disgust at his father. "You are pathetic. I never want to see you again."

"There it is. I was waiting for you to say that. And let's see if you know what happens next?"

"Fuck off!"

Nova turned and threw his door open, slamming it against the wall. Even as he ran away, out of the house and into his car, he could still hear the twisted laughs of his father and the same words shouted repeatedly: "And there he goes! But I won't leave you."

Nova dug into his pocket and fished out the bottle of Zoloft. He could feel himself teetering on the edge again, an edge that if he crossed, it would have terrible results as he had never been there. With shaking hands, he tried to tip a single pill into his hand, but in his trembling rage, he practically tipped the entire bottle.

"Fuck!" Nova yelled.

He grabbed a bunch and shoved them into his mouth, crunching the dry pills into a powder that soaked up every inch of moisture. Ignoring the horrible taste, he pulled a nearly empty plastic water bottle from the floor and drowned the pills.

Nova started his almost brand-new truck and sped out of the driveway. His father's voice was still echoing in his head, but as he drove toward the hills, the pills started to take effect, and a sweet silence settled, leaving him dreamy and numb. It was lucky that the hour was so late, for Nova swerved almost drunkenly up the Hollywood hills, muttering nonsense to himself until he finally reached the empty mansion that had been left to him.

He parked the truck haphazardly and stumbled into the house, climbing the stairs, walking past his bedroom, and collapsing in the vacant sheets of his dead grandfather's bed, still fresh with the memory of his ghost before deciding to go to the bathroom to vomit.

CHAPTER FIVE

Final Wishes

Three years ago

Bernie knew that old age was beginning to take its toll on him. Darkness that never existed before now crept around every corner of his subconscious, and he would often lose himself for hours, even days at a time, coming back to his senses in strange places, surrounded by piled objects and strings of disjointed newspaper clippings and photographs. There were days when his mind whirred at a thousand miles an hour, while other days, it moved like an aging snail. The genius he once possessed had evaporated like it never existed.

In those brief moments of clarity, he could plan, invent, and formulate complex theorems in his mind. It was a state of total logic and cold calculations. This was how he had spent most of his life; in the bliss of adoration and public glory. However, as age crept up on him more and more, he found those days of inspiration becoming fewer and fewer. Soon, the man who made science cool in inner cities and performed genetic experiments to test the limits of nature could barely roll himself out of bed. And, like a pendulum, he swung to extreme states of emotional quotient. It was here where the consequences of his decisions–career over family–left him drowning in guilt and remorse and, most of all, deep loneliness.

When he received his medical diagnosis, he was relieved. First came the early-onset Alzheimer's, then cancer. Alzheimer's and lung cancer would be bad news to most, but Bernie saw them as a saving grace. His way out. An opportunity to wipe the slate clean. And he didn't know how much longer he could hold on without ending his own life to avoid being an emotional burden on the family he now realized he had emotionally neglected over the years. Bernie had never had to deal with emotions before. Emotions were not for scientists. There were only facts and probability. At least, that was what he had thought. And ironically, he was so busy building his empire that he forgot to see a doctor for nearly fifty years.

There were few things left to live for. In fact, there was only one. Nova. For some reason, Bernie had developed an uncharacteristic fondness for the boy. To Bernie, Nova resembled himself in balance. And Nova had taken a fondness for Bernie. Nova's father, Eric, was the sort of man you could never rely on. Nova had found a father elsewhere. Bernie.

As the sun was setting over the Los Angeles hills one night, Nova decided to forgo dinner with his mother to visit his grandpa. By now, Nova was eighteen and had enough sovereignty to make decisions like that, even if it meant getting an earful later from his dad. Bernie had always encouraged him to prioritize family and friends and not become distracted by things that did not matter in old age.

It was a beautiful drive up the hills. Long, nicely paved, winding roads snaked upwards, growing denser with trees and million-dollar mansions around every turn. A great open view of L.A. below gave Nova a fresh sense of perspective from his everyday troubles.

Nova rang the doorbell when he arrived, watching the last rays of sun sink below the horizon. After a couple of minutes, no one had come to greet him. He frowned and tested the door handle. It opened with a soft click.

"Grandpa Bernie?" Nova called out.

His voice rang emptily through the large mansion. There was no response, causing an instant sense of panic to rise through his body. Nova had called ahead to make sure Bernie knew he was coming.

"Popsi?!" He called out again.

Nova heard a faint croak coming from upstairs. Nova's blood turned cold, and he burst into a sprint toward the sound. He found his grandfather on the floor, coughing up blood into a delicate white handkerchief.

"Popsi! Are you okay? What's going on?"

Nova ran to his side and helped the old man to his feet. He was heavier than he looked, and Nova struggled to carry him the short distance to his bed.

"I'm sorry..." Bernie coughed up more blood. "It's nothing, really."

"No, this isn't nothing. I'm calling an ambulance."

"No!" Bernie exclaimed, which sent him into an even greater coughing fit. "No ambulance. They'll tell the press." His breath was ragged and wheezing like someone was dragging sandpaper over rock.

"Grandpa, I can't leave you like this."

"Florence..." Bernie pointed with a quivering hand to a desk at the far end of his giant bedroom. "Call Florence."

Nova rushed over to the desk and rifled through the stack of scribbles and mathematical notations.

"First drawer." Bernie coughed.

Nova yanked it open and called the number on a platinum white business card. Dr. Florence Watkins. Almost twenty minutes later, a tall woman in her early fifties wearing scrubs and a braided coil bun hairstyle strode through the door.

Nova watched in fear as the doctor administered a spectrum of tests, pulling an oxygen tank from one of Bernie's closets and hooking the old man up to beeping machines that Nova never knew Bernie had. Dr. Watkins spoke to Bernie with kindness and care, casually bringing up past visits. Bernie's room had been transformed into a medical suite, and an intravenous drip was plugged into one of his grandfather's arteries.

Nova watched it all unfold in confusion. He hadn't known his grandfather was sick. Bernie had never said a word about his health, and Nova never asked. After a long while, Dr. Watkins finally pulled off her gloves and approached Nova, who was now sitting in a crimson armchair at the far end of the room. Dr. Watkins had a somber look on her face. Nova stood to meet her.

"The famous Nova Crenshaw." Dr. Watkins reached out to shake Nova's hand. "You did well to call me," Dr. Watkins said. "Another twenty minutes, and Grandpa might not have made it."

"What? What are you talking about? What's wrong with him?" Nova asked incredulously.

Dr. Watkins paused to analyze Nova's expression. "Son, your grandfather has stage four lung cancer."

Nova was speechless. He turned his gaze to his grandfather's frail body, all hooked up to an oxygen mask, eyes open but distant, like he was a world away.

"How long have you..." Nova gulped. "How long has he had this?"

"We diagnosed him over two years ago. He refused chemotherapy. And to be honest, I don't blame him."

"No!" Nova interrupted. "No, no, no!" Nova felt a rush of sadness explode through him. "Wait, how long does he have left?"

"Oh." Dr. Watkins looked away for a moment, then back to Nova. Their eyes met, and Nova knew instantly what the doctor was about to say. "It could be any day now, son."

"Any day!?" Nova sat back down.

"It gets aggressive at the end."

Dr. Watkins nodded solemnly and proceeded to pack up her tools. She was exiting the door when she stopped and turned back around. "Nova, your grandfather spoke at my high school almost forty years ago. I saw him and thought, *wow, look what's possible. Who is this man with an afro talking about science?* You should know that he's impacted a lot of lives and shifted our understanding of DNA mapping and eugenics. He's the reason I do what I do."

Dr. Watkins continued, "Don't hesitate to call if his situation worsens. There are plenty of things we can do to ease the transition for him."

Nova nodded without looking up.

"And just know that your grandfather loves you so much. I know more about you than I should." She laughed. "And frankly"–she paused–"it's all love."

And with that, the doctor left. Nova faintly heard the front door closing, but he didn't consciously register it. His body was shaking slightly, and a cold numbness was spreading to his limbs and taking over the thoughts in his head. The beeping of his grandpa's machine was miles away, and the strange sound of ragged breathing through the respirator was even further. Nova sat motionless for what seemed like hours. He couldn't bring himself to stand up, let alone leave. So, he just sat. He sat until the numbness of his mind pulled him into an uncomfortable sleep.

Nova awoke many hours later to the sound of birds singing. The sound of birds and the constant beep of the medical machine. It took him a moment to remember where he was, and he winced at the strain in his neck from sleeping upright for the entire night. He rubbed at his weary eyes and looked over to the sight of his grandpa in his bed for the first time since the doctor had left. Bernie's skin sunk deeply into the hollow of his jaw.

Nova looked away and instinctively went for his phone. It was early, just after seven in the morning. He scrolled through several missed calls from his mother and an angry text from his father. *Did they know Bernie was sick?* he wondered. Lennox was nowhere to be seen, which was strange. For as long as Nova had known his grandfather, Lennox had always been by the old man's side.

Nova shook off the strange feeling and took a cup of black coffee to the outside railing next to the pool, which looked out over the stretching streets and buildings of L.A. He watched the traffic from a distance and imagined all the different types of people going about their lives, each having to deal with their own myriad of struggles. For a moment, fantasies about the lives of strangers helped him not to feel so alone.

The coffee did little to change his mood. He left the cup half-drunk on the kitchen counter, taking the stairs to the room Bernie had saved for him. He sat for a very long time on the floor of the shower, letting the hot water bring feeling back into his bones. He couldn't say how long it took, but as the steady stream of water poured, the first wave of tears escaped in shaking sobs. Bernie was dying. And he had been dying for some time now. Nova pulled his knees close to his chest and cried. It started small and muffled and grew louder into near screams from the deepest part of his being. The shower rained down on him, leaving his skin blue and dark purple, steam filling up the small bathroom.

Nova had no other family to lean on. Stella had clocked out of reality years ago. She spent most of her time drinking wine, getting injectable face fillers, and getting high on benzos. And his father, Eric... Well, he was Eric. Nova had his loyal friends, but his friends could not fully comprehend the relationship he had with his grandfather. To them, he was just a famous old man that gave his grandson everything. There was no one. Nova had no one. Only Bernie. And maybe Lennox. But Bernie, Bernie was dying.

The realization that his family had become fragmented and dysfunctional sent him into another sobbing fit. *When did it start? Who is to blame?* Every answer Nova found led to ten more questions. He remained in the shower until the water began to run lukewarm. After almost an hour, Nova turned the shower off and gathered what little energy he had left to dress and pull himself together.

Finally, he made himself walk back to his grandfather's bedroom, which was bigger than most apartments. He stood on the border of the doorway, watching his grandfather. Bernie was awake, and he turned slowly at the sound of approaching footsteps.

"Lennox, are you back?"

"No. It's me."

"Nova... Oh, son, I'm sorry you have to see me like this."

Nova didn't respond. He just stood looking down at the floor with his arms folded. Bernie coughed, which made Nova look up. There was a pitcher of water on his bedside table with an empty glass. Nova sighed and walked over to it automatically, filling it up and helping his grandfather to sit up enough so that he could take a drink. Childhood memories flashed before his eyes as he gently removed the oxygen mask and eased the water and straw up to his grandfather's mouth.

It didn't go down easily. There was more spluttering than drinking. Eventually, Bernie raised his hand, signaling Nova to stop.

"That's enough," he said wearily.

Nova put the glass down and pulled a chair over to the bedside. The two sat in silence for a long while.

"When were you going to tell me?" Nova finally said.

Bernie gazed shamefully into Nova's eyes. "I wasn't."

Nova shook his head in disbelief.

"I thought it would be better that way," Bernie mumbled. "I didn't want you to see me suffering."

"Well...I have now."

Bernie nodded.

"Does Eric know?"

Bernie looked at Nova incredulously. "I haven't spoken to your father for more than two minutes for almost four years." He then proceeded to cough for a good minute. "I wouldn't be able to stand that slime ball trying to weasel his way into my will anyways."

Nova's jaw clenched even harder, and he smirked. "That's why you didn't tell me either, isn't it?"

"No, Nova. No. How could you think that?"

"I don't believe for one second that you kept this from me just because you didn't want me to see you suffering. Maybe dad is right; there's always some agenda with you."

Nova stood and stormed over to the far window. He suddenly found himself furious with his grandfather. He had to get away from the man, or he might pull the plug on his oxygen.

"Damn it, Nova! Don't make me shout!" Bernie began to cough.

"Then why don't you tell me the fucking truth!" Nova yelled back. "Maybe I could have saved you."

"Save me? Relax your ego?"

"You keep people so far away from you. You think you're protecting yourself, but you're hurting people who love you." Nova could barely find the words to express his love for his stubborn grandfather.

"Fine!" Bernie coughed and gasped for a breath of air.

"I hid it from you because I am ashamed," he said, coughing. "I am ashamed I am dying, okay? You think I'm perfect, but I'm just a man. I'm not like you. I may deserve this."

Nova took a deep breath and turned back to face Bernie, his anger dissipating as quickly as it arose. The man looked like a pile of bones. A rush of feelings surged through Nova, and he found himself on the verge of tears again.

"I am sorry, Nova," Bernie whispered. "You are right. I should have told you. I am a fool."

Nova closed the distance between them and resumed his seat by Bernie's bed, taking his grandfather's hand in his.

"I'm sorry too. I shouldn't have yelled. I just don't know what I am going to do without you."

Bernie let out a low, wheezing scoff of a laugh. "Oh, please, son. I am as much of a bastard as your father. He doesn't think I know where I went wrong, but I do. I was too young and focused on my career. We didn't have shit growing up. I failed him."

"No, you didn't."

"Yes, Nova." There was a pause. "I have made some questionable decisions in my life."

Nova's brows furrowed. "With my dad?"

"All of it."

Bernie looked away, and his eyes seemed to gloss over in memory. His breath was shallow, and to Nova, it was like watching an invisible weight take over his grandfather.

"A woman came to me in the shadows. We made a deal. A horrible deal." Bernie's face scrunched in horror. "I thought what I was doing would be good in the long run. I see now that the end never justifies the means. Maybe cancer is my karma."

Nova listened in silence. *What is he talking about? Is this Alzheimer's?* Nova thought. Bernie would often confuse names and change subjects abruptly as he aged. He had drifted into a world of his own. Suddenly, Bernie's eyes came back into focus, and he shook himself out of the past.

"Yes, a woman," he said, looking off to a photo of his late wife. "I left you the mansion," Bernie whispered.

Nova frowned even deeper. "What?"

"Just don't sell it. Don't ever sell it..."

"Grandpa... What are you saying?"

"Promise me!" Bernie gripped Nova's hand fiercely, and his eyes were ablaze with severity.

"Okay, okay. I promise."

Bernie's grip relaxed.

82

"It's all yours. Everything."

Nova was speechless. He didn't know what to say. Thank you didn't come close.

He couldn't find the muscles to move his mouth.

"I left something to your mother too. She will have plenty. It is the least I can do."

Nova slumped into the back of his seat as the realization of what Bernie was saying finally took root.

CHAPTER SIX

Down the Rabbit Hole

Present day

Pearl screamed bloody murder as she and Nova were tackled to the ground. Her screams tore at her throat in guttural, wrenching curdles of sound. Tears flowed from her eyes as she scratched and kicked and bit at the force holding them down. Nova was fighting, throwing wild punches, and scrambling like a fish out of water.

That was until they heard its voice.

"Guys! Guys! It's me! Stop! It's me!"

Nova opened his eyes to see Ruben pinning them to the ground. His face was scratched in multiple places where Pearl's nails had landed. By his side, Magenta held her hand over her mouth in fear. Nova was panting in exertion as he became aware of his friends.

"What...?" Nova twitched, shaking his head and trying to process what was happening. Pearl stopped her struggle, and Ruben finally let his grip come loose.

"What the fuck is going on?" Ruben asked, standing up over them.

Nova and Pearl looked at one another, then back the way they had come. The forest was empty. Magenta watched them in shock. Pearl managed to point into the darkness, but neither she nor Nova could form the words to speak.

Ruben knew how to handle his drugs, and their hysteria did little to faze him. He had seen worse before. Hell, one of his ex-girlfriends had tried to stab herself while tripping. He had jumped in just in time to catch the knife before it plunged into her stomach. He had a big scar on his palm to show for it.

Ruben helped Pearl get to her feet. She was trembling and still looking frantically around to the darkened hills for signs of danger. Magenta rushed over to her and wrapped a blanket over her shoulders, guiding her inside. Nova was still lying breathless on the ground. Ruben crouched down and offered his shoulder to help Nova up. Together they made their way back to the safety of the mansion.

Magenta made warm chamomile tea and put tranquil music over the speakers. Pearl and Nova were both wrapped in blankets on the couch by the fireplace. It took almost an hour for them to be able to speak again.

"We saw something in the forest, right?" Nova finally muttered.

Pearl's eyes were wide as she looked into the fire, sipping softly on her tea.

"Saw what?" Ruben asked.

The image of a man with scratched-out eyes, drooling, flashed before both Nova and Pearl's eyes. Nova shook his head.

"A man," Pearl whispered.

Magenta exchanged a look with Ruben. "Are all the doors locked?" she asked.

He nodded yes. "What kind of man?"

Nova shook his head. "He had no eyes...just sockets and, like, syrupy blood."

"What the fuck...?" Magenta sagged against the back of the couch.

"You *both* saw him?" Ruben continued with his questioning.

Pearl and Nova nodded.

"As clear as you are standing in front of us," Pearl added.

"I've never heard of two people hallucinating the same thing," Magenta whispered in contemplation.

"Me neither," Ruben responded. "What else did you see?"

"Dead things." Pearl was starting to cry again. "Like digging themselves up from the ground. Like dirty hands reaching through the grass." Ruben looked at Magenta, then back to the two traumatized friends.

"I would say you were both just having the worst trip of your life."

"We saw something too," Magenta said, almost choking on her words.

Nova's head snapped in her direction. "What!?"

Magenta swallowed a lump in her throat. By now, the peak of their drugs was wearing off. Reality was still a little shaky but solid enough for them to formulate lucid thoughts and sentences.

"Ruben and I were...Well, we were in the middle of adult matters when we heard something from upstairs. At first, we thought that you had both come back and snuck into one of the bedrooms."

Pearl looked down at her scratched-up feet.

"Then we heard doors slamming in the whole house. One by one."

Ruben continued, "To be honest, I didn't think anything of it."

"That's when I saw them," Magenta said.

"*Them*?" Nova asked. His body was quivering again from the memory of the eyeless man.

"Two little boys...they looked like twins, maybe?" Magenta whispered, pointing out to where the pool was. "They were just standing there...Watching us...I pulled something over myself, and they were looking right at me. Almost like they were drugged or something. It was..."

88

"I thought Magenta was being crazy," Ruben interrupted. "Then... I saw them too. Two little Negritos. Little pervs couldn't have been older than, like, ten."

Nova's heart froze. An old feeling began to percolate in the depths of his unconscious.

"For fucks sake..." Pearl couldn't hold back her tears. "What are we even still doing here?!"

Magenta pulled her in close and coaxed her with gentle shhs.

"None of us are sober enough to drive down these hills right now," Ruben said. "And if we get stopped...umm, none of us are white. If LAPD is anything like Inglewood PD, then"- Ruben motioned his fingers like a gun-"pow, pow. Ask questions last."

"All right, I've heard enough!" Nova jumped in. "We were all trippin' balls, and we saw some weird shit. That's all there is to this. I think it is little more than coincidence, the fact that everything is normal now that we're sober. Look!"

Nova stood and unlocked the large glass doors, stepping out into the darkness of the pool deck. Los Angeles' forest whispered in the background.

"There is nothing out here! I've literally been coming to my grandpa's house ever since I was a baby, and this has never happened, but the second I drop acid with you fucks, all shit hits the fan!"

Pearl burst into an even greater wave of tears.

"Oh, for fucks sake, Pearl..." Nova was getting angry.

The anger was, of course, a façade. One to cover up the deep-seated fear that he had been drenched in only moments before. A knowing that had been attached to him his whole childhood. The twins had created a deep sense of déjà vu in Nova, a sense of familiarity and remembering. Nova knew who those twins were. Ruben glanced at Pearl and Magenta, then walked energetically to mediate the space between them and Nova.

"All right. Let's all just calm down and take some deep breaths." Ruben began to guide the group in deep breathing meditation. "Magenta, take Pearl upstairs. A shower will sober her up...I'm a professional stoner, okay?"

He then turned Magenta. "And can you tuck in your boob? It's distracting."

Magenta adjusted her tank top and guided Pearl up the stairs. Nova watched them as they disappeared around the bend.

"I shouldn't have brought you guys here..." Nova said, looking off toward downtown's city lights in the distance. "Lennox is on vacation, and I thought..."

Ruben rolled his eyes. "Stop being an asshole. Here, take this." He stretched out a hand with two pills in it.

"Fuck you. Are you serious? More drugs after all of this? I'm not taking another one of your pills, bro."

"It's 5-HTP," Ruben said dryly. "And this one is Klonopin. Nothing psychoactive. They help to calm me down if I've overdone it. We haven't drunk anything, so you don't have to worry about any weird side effects. It's natural, bro...for anxiety and to help you sleep. Read the label."

Nova looked at him with distrust.

"Look, man. I tripped so bad once, my dead brother came back to life. I followed him to the edge of a bridge. And I was going to jump before some rando pulled me down. I've been in this situation and seen it happen to people I love way too many times. That's the gamble you play when you take drugs like this. Let's call it a fine balance between...enlightenment and psychosis." He paused and held out his hand further. "Trust me; these will help."

Nova sighed and took the pills from Ruben's hand. He swallowed them dry without a second thought.

"See?" Ruben asked, raising his eyebrow. "You'll be falling asleep in half an hour, and we'll all wake up with a wild story to tell at the next sorority party." He smiled and smacked Nova's butt.

Nova nodded, looking down at the ground. "My bad, Rube. For, you know...saying that shit. I didn't mean it."

"Hey." Ruben pulled Nova in for a hug. "We're all good, bro. All love, bro."

Meanwhile, Pearl had stripped down and was seated on the shower floor. Magenta sat on the toilet in a daze. The water was like rainfall, coming directly from the ceiling. There was enough water pouring to fit another person in there comfortably without anyone having to push or take turns for a shower.

"Magenta?" Pearl whispered. A second showerhead was movable, and Magenta had unhooked it from the wall and gently applied its flow to the nape of Pearl's neck, noticing the scratches on Pearl's feet through the corner of her eye.

"I think the boys are right," Magenta responded, combing her fingers through Pearl's hair. "I'm so sorry. I thought the acid was pure, but it must have been laced with something for us to trip like that..."

Pearl was hugging her knees close to her chest. The warm water was helping to ground her mind and keep her emotions in check.

"I think I recognized that man," she whispered.

"Your subconscious probably just scraped that image up and played on your fears," Magenta assured her. "Those twins I saw looked just like those twins who had been kidnapped eleven years ago. Remember when we were kids?"

Pearl continued, "He looked like that CEO who went missing a while back. Except with...no eyes."

Magenta looked at Pearl suspiciously and continued speaking, "I remember my mom losing her shit. She wouldn't let me have a sleepover for ages. She couldn't stop thinking about them, and her fear rubbed off on me for the longest time. And twins are kinda rare, so...we never know what we are still holding onto until we do... I guess."

She paused. "Does that make any sense? Fuck, I still can hardly think straight."

Pearl managed a semblance of a laugh. "Yeah, that makes sense."

Magenta sat back against the slate of the shower walls. "Girl, what a night!"

"I'm really happy you were here," Pearl said softly. "I was on the verge of completely losing it."

Magenta grinned and hugged Pearl closely against her bare chest. "Anytime, boo. You know, sometimes people overthink things or make connections where there aren't any. We have to try to be present like the rest of the world, I guess..." Magenta rolled her eyes. Pearl giggled.

Nova found himself navigating the upper halls of the mansion with his eyelids drooping. He and Ruben had talked themselves into a sleepy haze, and the Klonopin had done its work in soothing their nerves. Nova stood in the doorway to his room. It was the same room he slept in as a child. The same single bed in the far-right hand corner, with the same Tetris print duvet cover and over-washed sheets. The memory of his grandfather danced with his benzo-muted emotions. Nova threw himself onto the bed and pulled out the bunny he had hidden underneath it, hugging it close to his chest. *Miss you, Grandpa. Every day,* he thought. Nova stared at the ceiling for a few seconds before sleep pulled him under.

Everything was dark for several hours. Nova's body was suspended in a deep, dreamless sleep, resting away from the drugs and night's strange events. But, when Nova did eventually awake, he was not in his bed. He was standing in a dark hallway that looked like an underground tunnel extending far out in front of him. At the end was an open door that his senses instinctively knew led to the basement. Nova's heart raced. He recognized this hallway. He knew that door. Nova suddenly remembered he was dreaming, and the awareness triggered the memory of the recurring nightmare he had as a young boy. His intuition sensed he had been here before, but he couldn't remember how the dream ended.

Feeling panicked, Nova tried to pull himself out of the dream. The sedating effect of the benzos had him locked in sleep paralysis. Nova pounded on the hallway walls. The walls were not solid, and he created surface waves with each hit that rippled down the hallway.

He turned around to see where he had come from, but there was a solid concrete wall behind him that inched closer with every step. A tang of hospital cleaning chemicals, phenyl and bleaching powder, wafted from the only open door at the end of the hallway, and it beckoned him like an angler fish in the depths of the sea. He finally arrived at the door at the end of the hallway to a descending stairwell.

At that moment, the hall closed in on itself. The walls moved closer together. Nova swore and tried to push them back, but they continued to press against him with an increasingly strong force. He faced the dark staircase, slamming and pounding the walls that splashed like water and trying everything he could to prevent the walls from compressing him into a mess of flesh and bone. He knew he had no choice. He would have to go back down those stairs to face whatever awaited him.

"Nova?" A woman's delicate voice called out in the distance. "Nova?"

* * *

Ruben had passed out on the couch. Magenta was the only one out of bed, having tucked Pearl in several hours ago. She wandered the silent mansion like a ghost, running her fingers along the walls, using the flashlight on her phone as a torch. The upstairs rooms had been primarily empty. Empty in the sense that there was nothing of interest, except for expensive furniture that belonged in a showroom. She had now found herself in one of the back rooms on the first floor adjacent to Lennox's quarters. The room looked like something out of the fifties. There was a large mahogany desk in the center, and every wall was covered floor to ceiling with packed bookshelves. She assumed, by the vintage style, that this must have been Nova's grandfather's study.

Dust appeared on her fingertips as she grazed along the spine of the books. Magenta was not a usual sort of human. She had spent most of her teenage years convinced that she was a witch and had even found herself within an occult circle that gathered in the basement of an esoteric bookstore. She knew things before they happened. Sometimes, she had a sense that she had met people before, all things that felt very real to her that others found unrelatable. While she had talked everything down as a 'bad trip' to Pearl, she herself didn't believe that for one second.

While she would never tell Nova, Pearl, or Ruben, she had seen things, visions, and forms of energy as a child, which had nearly driven her to a psychiatric hold. It wasn't that she didn't trust her friends; she just knew they weren't at a point to understand where she was coming from without concern. Her own mother hadn't understood. Magenta had spent most of her childhood in and out of psychologists and therapists' offices, diagnosed with all sorts of disorders. Visits triggered by her assertion that she was possessed and her siblings were portals. Only she knew the truth. That the things she saw were spirits, and if it wasn't for the people she had met in her occult group, she would still be on medication with weak senses and barely functioning.

Magenta felt something strange the moment she stepped into the mansion. She hadn't said anything because she had learned to keep her intuition to herself. And now, she was following the hunch and premonition like a compass. Magenta crouched down and opened the first drawer of the desk. It slid out easily. There was nothing more than a few envelopes, some loose paper clips, pens, and more than one wax press.

Magenta took out one of the wax presses and observed the engraved metal. In the center was a triangle with strange, unfamiliar symbols surrounding it. The other wax press revealed a crest with two C's poking out either side of a shield. Magenta noted that it was the same crested sigil she had observed on the ring that sat on Nova's pinky finger. Most likely, a family crest passed on from his grandfather.

"Why would you have two different sigils, Papa Crenshaw?" Magenta whispered out loud to herself.

She rummaged around a bit more in the first drawer but found nothing else of any particular interest. The second drawer was filled with a bunch of legal papers. There were some scribbles and scientific notations on loose scraps of paper that were as good as gibberish. She frowned and went for the third drawer. She gave it a gentle pull, and it slid a centimeter out before stopping. Magenta pulled again, but the jammed drawer wouldn't budge. It was locked.

She lowered the flashlight and caught the gold keyhole built into the mahogany. Slowly, she ran her magenta nails over an engraving above the lock. It was just like the first wax press she had seen. A triangle surrounded by small, unrecognizable symbols. Luckily, this was not Magenta's first rodeo. Her eyes lit up in challenge, and she quickly returned to the first drawer, fishing out two paper clips as adrenaline suddenly coursed through her blood.

She bent the paper clips into shape, just like her older sister had taught her, and fit them into the small keyhole. Closing her eyes, she felt within the lock with her two paper clip prongs. It was a simple lock. Seven spring-loaded pins. She just needed to find the right tension for each of them.

"Just a little nudge and..." Magenta whispered to herself. Moments later, there was a satisfying click, and she was in. Magenta was in her element. She never truly admitted how much satisfaction she got out of snooping around in places she was not welcome, but she couldn't deny the rush of excitement that surfaced knowing that she was doing something that she probably shouldn't be doing.

Her anticipation died quickly. The drawer was empty except for a single key.

"Dammit," she cursed as she picked the key out of the drawer.

However, the second she touched the key, a flash of strange feelings and emotions washed over her. She recoiled, and the key dropped back into the drawer with a hollow clang. Magenta shuffled back instantly, getting some distance from the desk. A wave of grief and horror was beating strong in her blood. She found herself in tears. Something was wrong. Oh, so wrong.

Magenta had felt things in objects before-traces, memories of what the object held. She had felt these things ever since she was little. But she had never felt anything like this. It was a dark, twisting corridor of emotions that spun her gut awry and told her to get as far away as possible. Now. This key might as well have unlocked the doors of hell. Magenta brought herself into check before she hyperventilated. She took long, deep breaths to calm the turbulence in her nervous system, sipping the air long, in and out, in and out. It took her a while to recover, but eventually, she gathered the courage to approach the desk again.

She needed to find out what Grandpa Bernie was hiding. Instead of going for the key, however, she tapped with her knuckles on the bottom of the desk drawer. She had heard the key fall and heard the hollow sound it made against the wood. Her suspicions were correct. As she knocked on the wood, she heard that same hollow sound. The drawer had a false bottom.

* * *

Nova was forced into the dark stairwell as the walls closed in behind him. He had to fight to turn and pound at the now sealed doorway. There was something down below, down where the stairs led. He could hear breathing; he could feel another presence. He knew he had faced it before, and whatever it was had scared him so much his mind had forced him to forget. But now, here he was, and there was no other choice but to descend into the depths. The sound of high heels came closer toward him. "Nova?"

* * *

Magenta nudged the false bottom of the drawer free with one of the pens she had found. The wood popped up with minimal effort. She tried to take the board out without the key touching her skin. She was not ready to feel those emotions again. Setting the thin plank of wood with the key on it down beside her, she picked up her phone again and shone it into the now unveiled drawer. There was a thick, unlabeled file, and on top of it was an old video cassette tape. Magenta held her breath as she picked up the paper file.

* * *

Nova was trembling as he slowly descended the dark passage. He took each step cautiously, one at a time, and with every step forward, the path back up sealed shut behind him like images being sucked into a black hole. He took another step, and his foot landed on a hard ground. He had reached the bottom. There was nothing to be seen. He could only feel the musty air, damp and rotten, with the subtle smell of bleach.

A single lightbulb flickered on in the middle of the room. Nova stumbled back and found himself hard-pressed against a wall. He shut his eyes tight, not wanting to see whatever the light was meant to illuminate. But closing his eyes made everything worse. Flashes of the faceless man scratched across his mind; he felt the man's heartbeat, dark and scarred and full of terror. He couldn't take it anymore. He forced his eyes open to escape the sight of the man's hollow, scratched-out eyes and violent neck movements.

The lightbulb flickered as Nova did, dancing shadows across a single hair tie bow, small and pink, in the empty room. And the memories of his childhood nightmares returned.

* * *

The file Magenta had found was full of faces she knew she should never have seen. Each face was dark and hollow. Faces of elderly to young adults, but mostly children. There were no names, just numbers. Like they were branded animals. The children...so many children. Magenta couldn't make sense of the words written at length beneath every face. They passed through her mind like sand through a sieve, and many of the sentences were covered in black blocks, obstructing the text from being read. Only some of the words registered. Genetic mutation. Extraterrestrial. Abducted. Crossbreed.

"What the fuck?"

Magenta's hands were shaking. She lifted the cassette tape and managed to read the label. "Cases 1-16." That was all it said. When Magenta was exploring the mansion, she had seen an old television with a cassette player connected to it. Her parents had owned one when she was a kid, and memories of watching *Alice in Wonderland* returned.

Magenta brought the file and tape to the other room and slipped it into the player. It took her a while to get it to work, but eventually, the television flickered on, and the tape played instantly. There was a dark room with a single table and two chairs. A young girl sat in one of the chairs. She wore what looked like a thin hospital gown, and her arms were cuffed to the table. A moment later, a man in a white lab coat approached her. Magenta squinted. *Grandpa Bernie?*

"Do you remember anything about the night you were taken?" the scientist said coldly.

The child was crying and shaking her head.

Magenta was in shock. She didn't know what she was watching. Her eyes were glued to the screen, and everything else in her surroundings blurred into nothing. That was when a noise came from behind her. Magenta screamed, and the files went flying from her hand. In an instant, she scurried to the other side of the room and pulled out a small pocketknife.

"Jesus! What the fuck, Magenta!"

It was only Ruben.

"Holy shit. Holy shit!" Magenta said as she realized that she wasn't about to be murdered.

"What the hell are you doing?" Ruben was rubbing his eyes and taking in the scene around him.

"I think Nova's grandpa was a crazy kidnapping psycho."

"What?" Ruben said as his eyes finally landed on the television. "What is that? Seriously?"

Magenta stood up and slowly approached Ruben.

"Hey, put that knife away, dude. I've had enough of this shit."

"Sorry." Magenta flicked the knife down and stashed it back in her pocket. "Look. Something is seriously wrong here. That's his grandpa, right?"

Scrambling onto her knees, she picked up the sheets of paper that she had sent flying only a moment ago. "Look at these."

Ruben didn't look impressed. "It's fucking three in the morning. You look like a scared deer with pink hair."

"Look at them!" Magenta said insistently, shoving the papers into Ruben's chest. "I found them in Nova's grandpa's study."

"Damn, Magenta. What were you doing snooping around? You know Nova is touchy and super protective about his grandpa."

"Jesus, Ruben, will you just look at the damn papers!?"

Ruben looked at Magenta's wild eyes and then back at the stack of files in his hand. He sighed and walked over to one of the leather chairs and sat down.

Magenta crouched in a corner of the room, biting her nails and watching with unblinking eyes as Ruben read through the files. After a long while, Ruben looked up and stared at the tape still playing on the old television screen. He looked back down at the papers in his lap, then finally over at Magenta. Their eyes locked, and a cold tension passed between them. Ruben couldn't find the words to speak. Neither could Magenta. They sat in silence for a very long time until the sound of footsteps approached.

Both sat up with alertness, and their eyes darted toward the door. A pair of scratched-up feet stepped into view, and Pearl stood before them, dressed in a large t-shirt, her arms huddled across her chest.

No one said a word. Pearl's eyes had skipped over Magenta and Ruben and were glued to the black and white recording playing on the screen. While Ruben had been reading the files, the tape had progressed to several different people, each cuffed to that same table and each undergoing the same fire of questions.

Pearl raised a shaking finger at the television screen. "What... What is that?"

"Pearl..." Magenta tried to speak.

"That's him," Pearl interrupted.

"What?" Magenta asked.

"The man on the screen—that famous CEO. That's who I saw."

Pearl slowly approached the television and traced the contours of the handcuffed man seated across from the person in the lab coat.

"Where did you get this?" Pearl said in a choked whisper.

Magenta and Ruben looked at one another.

"Where did you get this!" Pearl demanded.

"Hey, calm down." Ruben stood up and reached for Pearl's arm.

But Pearl yanked her arm away and continued to point at the television. "You better fucking tell me, or I swear I'm going to lose it."

"I found it," Magenta said.

"Where?" Pearl repeated through clenched teeth.

"In Nova's grandpa's study," Magenta admitted.

Pearl went blank as her brain tried to process the information. She took a couple of steps away and had to sit down on one of the chairs.

Magenta glanced helplessly at Ruben.

"You told me it was just a bad trip," Pearl finally said.

"I know... I..." Magenta tried to explain herself.

"You told me I was just making it all up!"

"Pearl..."

"Did you?!"

Magenta looked down to the ground. "I'm sorry."

"What the fuck!" Pearl shouted.

"Hey!" Ruben interjected. "Calm down, Pearl. You were one step away from a full-on psychosis. None of us could have known that Nova's grandpa was some psycho."

"We have to get the fuck out of here," Pearl said absently. "We have to..." Her eyes suddenly darted up. "What if Nova..."

"Oh, shit..." Ruben interrupted, realizing what Pearl was about to say.

"Don't say it," Magenta warned.

"Say it, Pearl!" Ruben responded.

"What if Nova lured us up here to do something to us?"

"Oh, my God," Magenta interjected.

"Umm, nice story, but... Nova is black," Ruben said.

"Okkkkkay...." Pearl continued, "Sadistic black people exist..." She pointed to the screen. "Clearly!"

"Exactly! Nova is black." Ruben clapped. "Which is why both of you need to relax. Can you show me any black, Mexican, or Korean into shit like this? No, you can't! Plus, Nova? Nova can barely kill a daddy longlegs. You guys, I won't have you talk about my best friend like this."

* * *

Nova's eyes shot open. He was drenched to the bone in sweat, and his heart was beating like a mad racehorse.

Suddenly, all the nightmares he had as a child came rushing back. How had he forgotten? They had been such a big part of his life. He tried to breathe and found his mouth thick and parched from dryness. Stumbling out of bed, he descended the stairs and turned on the kitchen sink, forgoing a glass and sticking his mouth directly under the stream of water coming from the luxurious faucet.

Having heard a noise, Ruben slowly walked out of the room with Magenta's knife in his hand. The friends crept down the hallway as Nova moved around the kitchen. Ruben peeked around the corner to see a shirtless Nova drinking like he had spent forty days in the desert. Ruben motioned for Pearl and Magenta that the area was clear.

"Nov?"

Nova turned around in panic, fear plainly written on his face.

"Nova, are you okay?"

Nova looked at Ruben, then down to his hand. Seeing his friend's worried reaction, Ruben cursed and tucked the knife away as quickly as he could.

"Nova, what happened?"

"Nnnnnightmare," Nova managed to stutter. He was still recovering from the trauma of being trapped in his dream. Nova's dreams and emotions always reached a state of unanimity when he slept, which night after night created harsh tears in Nova's sense of reality. He had gone to therapy and seen countless counselors and psychiatrists. Only his grandfather could comfort him.

Ruben closed the distance between them and pulled Nova in close for a hug. Nova's arms dangled by his sides as Ruben held him tightly, and in the embrace, Nova sobbed. Ruben met Magenta and Pearl's eyes, gesturing for them to join. In that moment, all suspicion that Pearl had planted about Nova possibly being an accomplice in his grandfather's lunacy vanished. Magenta watched the doubt disappear from Pearl's face at the sight of Nova crying in Ruben's arms, and they all surrounded their friend and held him close until he stopped.

After Nova regained his composure, Magenta, Pearl, and Ruben explained what they were doing and what had been found. Nova listened without saying a word. He reviewed the files. He watched the tape. When everything was said and done, the friends looked at one another with apprehensive glances. All except for Nova. He was staring blankly into space. Strange fragments of memories were shooting in and out of his mind, disappearing as soon as they arrived, more like dreams than anything else. Their evanescence made it all the harder for Nova to think. A part of him was still there, but his body had gone numb, and he felt distant like he was outside of himself and watching everything happen from a third-person point of view.

"Nova, are you with us, bud?" Ruben asked.

Nova's mouth was dry again.

"Let me get this straight," Nova finally said. His voice was raspy and devoid of any emotions. "You went spying around my grandfather's house, broke a lock, and now you think that he is the L.A. Love Hunter based on some redacted files and an old tape with no context?"

Pearl, Magenta, and Ruben exchanged guilty glances.

Magenta put her arm around Nova. "We didn't say anything about him being the Love Hunter, Nova..."

Nova realized what he had said.

"K-" He cleared his throat and tried again. "Key."

Ruben frowned. "What?"

Nova turned to face Magenta directly. "The key that you found. Where is it?"

Magenta stuck two fingers into her pocket and pulled it out. Nova looked it over a couple of times, then clenched it in his fist.

"I know what door it opens."

CHAPTER SEVEN

The Cabin

Present

"Uh uh. No way. I'm not going back out there," Pearl said as Nova led them to the back door.

"Would you rather stay here by yourself?" Magenta muttered, folding her arms matter-of-factly.

"No. But why are those our only two options? What are we still doing here? We are all sober enough to drive. Let's fucking go! Now!"

Nova turned around abruptly. There was anger written plain on his face. "You know what! Maybe you *should* all just get out of here! You all seem to think I come from a kidnapping murderer, so just go and leave me the fuck alone. Happy Birthday, Nova, signed your

111

fake ass friends. Oh, and call the cops if you want! None of this would have happened if you hadn't come!"

Pearl recoiled slightly at the outburst.

"Hey, come on, Nov. I know it must be hard to hear all these things," Ruben said calmly. "I can't imagine if..."

"You can't imagine. None of you can. This man was *my grandfather*! He took care of me when no one else did! He was a good man. He did more in his life than any of you will ever do."

"Nova. Your grandfather was experimenting on people... Or at least I think they were people..." Magenta said in a tone that cut straight to the facts. "History books call this medical torture."

"Maybe they were criminals or spies!" Nova retorted. "My grandfather said he worked for some government organization at one point in his life."

"Your grandfather was a geneticist. And most of the people on the files were children, Nova," Magenta said softly, trying to calm him down. "Kids."

The memory of the twins in his class flashed before his eyes. And the nightmare of the striped, blue suspenders, in that eerily similar dark room where he had descended. That shut him up. On some level, he knew just as his friends did that something was very wrong, but he wasn't ready to admit it out loud, let alone to himself.

"Look, man." Ruben took a step toward Nova. "We know this all sounds crazy, but if your grandfather is innocent, then you will have nothing to worry about. And we sure as hell aren't going to leave you alone up here. Not if what you and Pearl saw out here was real. But one thing's for sure; we need to see where that key leads to."

"Fine," Nova said. "I'll take you there, but you're going to feel pretty stupid."

"I don't *need* to see. I *need* to go home," Pearl said agitatedly. "Ruben!" Pearl called out. Shouldn't we all be running the fuck away, like, why are we trying to willfully kill ourselves in a *dungeon* in a dark *forest?*"

Nova opened the back door and stormed out at a quick pace, moving very pointedly toward the trees. Ruben followed directly after him, and Magenta was taking a step forward when Pearl grabbed her arm.

"Magenta. I have a really bad feeling about this. Everything in my gut is telling me that we need to get the hell out of here."

Magenta took in the fear from Pearl's eyes and offered her a sympathetic smile, brushing a loose strand of hair away from her face.

"I have a similar feeling," Magenta whispered back. She took some time to look around the house. "This place gave me the creeps the moment I stepped in. But Nova's grandpa is dead now. Whatever messed up shit he was up to is over. And remember, ghosts can't harm us."

"Magenta... Please."

"Come on." She took Pearl's hand. "Let's see where that key leads to. And if any more ghosts pop up, Ruben and I will take care of them. It's not the first time I've had to fight off a spirit from another realm." Magenta giggled lightly.

Pearl met Magenta's eyes reluctantly and was mildly disgusted. Magenta squeezed her hand, and they walked off into the dark to catch up with Nova and Ruben.

"Where the hell are we going?" Ruben asked Nova as they wound through the trees. Pearl and Magenta were close behind.

"Grandpa's cabin," Nova replied. "His work shed."

"More like murder shed," Magenta muttered to Ruben.

Nova heard her and shot her a pointed glare.

"Just saying..."

Ruben nudged her.

Ignoring Magenta's comment, Nova continued speaking. "After he retired, he took up *woodworking*. Almost every time I came to visit, he would surprise me with a new toy. Look, there it is." Nova pointed ahead with his flashlight.

"Why would your grandfather keep a key to a woodworking shed locked in a drawer in his study?" Ruben asked.

"I don't know! He probably had some expensive tools in there and didn't want any rogue hiker snooping around."

Nova angrily slipped the key into the lock and threw the door open, indicating with his hand that the cabin was all theirs to explore. Ruben, Magenta, and Pearl all swapped worried looks.

"Are you serious? You're nosy *and* scared?" Nova exclaimed. "Fine. I'll go in first. You're all a bunch of assholes."

Nova disappeared into the crevices of the cabin, and a moment later, a dim light flickered on. Ruben was the first to approach, the wooden floorboards creaking under his weight.

"Wait," Pearl whispered, pulling Magenta back. "We can't go in there. I don't know how I know, but I just do."

"Pearl, I'm scared too. But whatever is in there, we will face it together."

"Magenta! You aren't listening. Wake up," Pearl said in a hushed exclamation, snapping in Magenta's face.

"Look." She pulled out her phone. There were three bars of signal. "If we see anything messed up in there, we'll call the cops straight away and get the fuck out of here. Okay?"

That seemed to calm Pearl down. "Okay."

A second later, Ruben appeared in the doorway. "It looks like a regular old woodworking shed to me."

Magenta frowned. "What?"

Nova stepped out behind Ruben. "I fucking told you."

Magenta avoided Nova's eyes and pushed past him into the shed. She did a quick survey of the place. They were right. It was just an old cabin connected to a woodworking shed. Magenta frowned and closed her eyes. Something wasn't adding up.

"This doesn't make sense," she said out loud.

"Wow. Now that you've been proven wrong, you can't even admit it."

She rolled her eyes. "No." She gestured her arms at the little shed. "This space is tiny. The dimensions don't add up."

Pearl had walked in at this point, her arms crossed tightly over her chest. "Magenta's right," she said softly. "The width from the outside is at least twenty, thirty feet more."

"This is hardly ten deep," Magenta confirmed.

As they were speaking, Ruben disappeared outside. Nova, on the other hand, was getting angrier.

"You are just making shit up now. My grandpa was a good man! Why are you so determined to make him look bad just because you found a tape? You couldn't even see who that scientist was clearly. And if it was him, I'm sure he was *helping* those people!"

Magenta was beginning to doubt herself. Maybe she had jumped to conclusions too quickly. But...that feeling she had when she touched the key. She had learned to trust her senses, but they were making her look like quite the fool right now. "I could have been wrong..."

At that moment, Ruben appeared back in the doorway. "The girls are right. The cabin's almost double the size on the outside than it is in here."

"Hah! I knew it," Magenta said triumphantly.

Pearl, on the other hand, stood motionless. The pit in her stomach was gnawing at her, and she had goosebumps on every inch of her skin. She tried to brush the feeling aside, but every sound and creak and gust of wind through the trees had her eyes neurotically flicking from side to side. With the news that Ruben had just brought, the hairs on the back of her neck rose even higher.

"Oh, for fuck's sake." Nova stormed out of the shed, his head pounding wildly. "Take your time. I'll be out here when you decide to come to your senses!"

"Jesus," Magenta whispered. "I hope we're wrong about all this. Poor Nova. If any of y'all came for my family like this, I would never forgive you."

Nova sat on the edge of the steps leading up to the cabin. He could hear his friends whispering. He didn't know what they were saying, but he knew they were talking about him. His head hurt, and he could hardly think straight. In all the times he visited his grandpa, he had never come out here. He had only seen it a couple of times while exploring.

A distant memory tried to fight its way into Nova's head. His grandfather was yelling. It was probably the only time he had seen his grandfather angry. Bernie had caught Nova peering into one of the cabin's windows. At that age, Nova was used to being yelled at by his father over things that didn't really make sense to him. Like in school when he misspelled a word or was caught daydreaming. Even

117

touching the wrong thing in his house sent his father into a fury.

Like many kids, Nova had learned that children are not respected and are inferior in the eyes of adults. He had coped by keeping his head low and doing his best to stick to the rules. That worked for the most part.

He tried to push the memory away and clear his head, but strange images kept returning. Lennox dragging a huge white trash bag of sorts filled with something heavy. His grandfather sometimes disappearing for hours at a time with no explanation.

No. No. No.

He clenched his eyes shut and dug the palms of his hands into his sockets.

"Hey guys, come take a look at this," Magenta said.

Ruben put down the toolbox he was rifling through and went over to her side. She was crouched low to the ground and looking at something on the wooden floor.

"What is it?" Ruben asked.

"See these scuff marks? Here, and there."

Ruben shone his light to see what Magenta was talking about.

"These kinds of marks only come around from repeatedly dragging something. See how the coat of primer has been removed, and you can see the discoloration of the wood?"

"No," Pearl said.

Magenta stood up and began to rearrange things around on the shelves in front of her.

"No way..." Ruben saw what Magenta was trying to get at.

Magenta moved a couple of framed pictures and some wooden figures and reached for a metal sculpting tool, but the tool stuck firmly to the wood. She went for it again. It stayed put.

She exchanged a look with Ruben, who was peeping over her shoulder. Then, taking a deep breath, she turned the sculpting tool. There was a click from somewhere behind the wall, and a light waft of air escaped through a crack in the shelf and wall, like an airplane door's airlock. Magenta followed the seam and pulled. And the entire shelf spun out like a door.

"That explains the drag marks," Magenta whispered.

"Holy shit!" Ruben said, hardly believing what he was seeing. "Nova's grandpa has a fucking secret dungeon."

Magenta spared a look toward the door before lighting up her phone's flashlight and opening the shelf door all the way. A cloud of dust poured out, and both Magenta and Ruben coughed as they inhaled a sweep of particles that smelled like antiseptic, dust, and soap.

"Man. Whatever this place is, it hasn't been used in a long time."

Pearl was standing far back. There was a wrench in her gut, twisting and hissing like an old stovetop kettle at boiling point. She felt frozen to the spot. Magenta, however, gathered her courage and took the first step. There was silence, then a muffled thump as Magenta backed into Ruben. A motion light had been triggered, and the entire back room was suddenly illuminated. This room was very different from the first. The other was messy and in disarray, but this one was in perfect tidiness. There was a desk with many shelves above it, each containing strange jars of fluid, and a neat stack of papers.

Pearl was motionless by the door, watching as Magenta and Ruben explored the secret room. She jumped as a sound came behind her. It was Nova. He had heard the scraping of wood, and as he stepped into the room, he froze beside Pearl. He could hear his own blood pumping in his ears, and the most terrifying sense of familiarity washed over him. Nova absently inched his way toward the room.

Magenta was inspecting one of the jars. She could barely make out the contents through the murky fluid.

"Are those..." Magenta tried to understand the floating particles and fragments. "Are those...eyes?"

Nova ignored his friends and walked straight toward a floor-to-ceiling mirror on the opposite side of the room. He was so out of it that he didn't even notice the shadow of his own reflection staring back at him. He laid a hand on the reflection, not knowing what he was doing.

Magenta gasped. "Oh, my God, Ruben, are these dicks in jars?"

Ruben floated over to Magenta. "Indeed, they are," he responded.

Then, in one swift movement, Nova ripped the mirror from the wall, which came crashing to the ground in a thousand splinters of razor glass shards. Pearl screamed, quickly covering her mouth and forcing the air back down her lungs.

"Fuck, Nova! What are you doing?!" Ruben shouted. "Trying to scare the shit out of us?"

Magenta was the only one who hadn't moved a muscle. She was staring exactly where Nova was, where the mirror had just been, and, instead of bare wood, there was a black iron door. Nova's breathing shifted into small, almost hyperventilating inhalations.

"Nova?"

He felt himself becoming light-headed. Ruben was by his side in an instant, with an arm around his friend's shoulder.

"Breathe, buddy. Just breathe. Deep breaths. That's it."

Nova had to fight against slipping into shock. The black iron door. He had seen it before. He had seen it many times over many years. It was the same door that had haunted his nightmares as a child.

And now, here it was, bare and exposed in the flesh of iron. And Nova knew exactly what he would find behind it. He would have to face a previously invisible truth about his grandfather once and for all.

CHAPTER EIGHT

The Iron Door

Ruben, Magenta, and Pearl all stood close together as Nova knelt in the shards of the shattered mirror. They glanced at one another with a mixture of shock and worry on their faces.

"Nov?" Ruben said slowly.

He took a couple of steps toward him, the soles of his shoes crunching against the broken mirror pieces.

"Stop!" Nova screamed.

Nova stood up and turned to face his friends. His eyes were mad and wild.

"I've had enough of this! You all need to go!"

"Nova," Ruben said, trying to calm his friend.

Nova's eyes darted to Ruben, who was still slowly approaching him.

"Don't come any fucking closer, or I swear to God, I'll kill you!" Nova picked up one of the shards of glass, gripping it tightly in his hand. Blood began to drip through his fingers.

He didn't even notice. His entire body was numb and tingling. He felt an entire world away.

"Nova, what the fuck?!" Ruben raised his palms defensively. "It's me! Calm down."

But Nova was in a world of his own. He prodded forward with the sharp mirror fragment in his hand.

"Stay back!"

"Holy shit, man! What the fuck?!" Ruben jumped back.

Pearl was trembling. "Look at his pupils," she whispered. "Is he going to kill us?"

"Like hell he is!" Ruben shouted.

Nova's eyes were dilated into giant black holes, so large that the brown and green of his irises were completely obscured. Magenta nodded and stepped forward past Ruben.

"Woah! Magenta, stay back! Nova's lost his mind!"

Magenta turned back to Ruben and met his eyes. "It's okay. I've got this." She turned back to face Nova. "Nova. Listen to me." Her voice was soothing, like a mother's coax.

Magenta had dealt with all sorts of crazy. From delusions to panic attacks, fits of rage, and manic episodes–she wasn't new to this game. Her mother was bipolar, and she had learned from an early age that it wasn't so much *what* you said that mattered but *how* you said it.

Words matter. Like a plucked guitar string, words carry vibrations. They carry feelings and emotions. And consequences. She could have said the most profoundly wise and assuring thing, but if she said it in the wrong way, it wouldn't mean anything. She let her words roll out like a silk and satin breeze.

"We're here with you. We're all here together. There is nothing to be scared about. We're with you."

Nova frowned, but already he was becoming less aggressive. Ruben turned and looked at Magenta like she was performing witchcraft. Which, in a way, she was. Very few people ever dive deeper than what's presented to them in the world. Magenta, on the other hand, had spent years researching ancient occult practices. She had spent years in dark basements and years learning from all sorts of people who would have been deemed insane by the mainstream collective. Now, with all this being said, she wasn't about to conjure a fireball, but she had soothed Nova's nerves enough to get close.

She laid her hand on his, the outstretched hand with the shard of mirror in it. Her gaze never left his. And in it there was no fear, no judgment.

She made sure all he could see was safety and love. Nova was not some insane person who had gone off his rocker; quite the opposite. He was an all-star. He was a stand-up guy. He was the person you leave a million-dollar mansion to because of his character and loyalty. He was in shock. And Magenta knew how to deal with shock. Her touch against his skin was light and intimate. It carried all the promise of warmth and a mother's bosom. Nova was still frowning at her, but his grip on the mirror shard loosened. He looked like a child lost at a carnival that never ended. Magenta smiled at him.

"It's okay. We're with you."

The mirror shard clattered to the floor, and Nova let out a breath he didn't even know he had been holding in. Suddenly, the room came into focus, and the first thing he saw was the blur of Magenta's eyes. His eyes moved down to the shattered mirror around him, then he raised his hands. He still couldn't feel anything, but he saw blood running from his palm.

"Take off your shirt, Ruben," Magenta said in an urgent whisper.

Ruben was still slightly stunned by the whole scenario. "What?"

"Take off your shirt!"

"Why? I don't think now is the right time for..."

"God, you're an idiot. It's for Nova's hand."

"Oh..."

Ruben quickly took off his shirt and handed it to Magenta. She ripped it a second later, tearing it in two.

"Hey! That was Supreme! It cost me like five hundos..."

Magenta threw him a glaring look that had Ruben almost cowering away. She quickly wrapped Nova's hand, making sure to keep a tight pressure to try and stop the bleeding.

"There. That should do it. For now, at least." She laid a bloody hand on his cheek. "How are you feeling?"

"What's going on?"

"We've had a big night, Nova. You're safe. I need you to stay calm. We're in your grandpa's cabin." Magenta was staring deep into Nova's eyes, pulling him out of the dark depths of his unconscious, pulling him back to the surface world.

"We're not allowed to be here," Nova said.

Pearl and Ruben exchanged looks of fear. Nova's voice had changed at that moment. Like he had become a child again.

"Why, Nova? Why are we not allowed to be here?"

The image of strange things floating in jars flashed through Nova's head. Blue suspenders. Stairs. Crying. Dark corridor.

His mind began to frazzle again.

"Nova," Magenta coaxed. "Stay with us. Do you know what's behind that door?"

"Door?"

Nova turned around and the dark iron practically screamed at him. A memory flashed of when he was a child. He was peering in through the window to the cabin.

A face. His grandfather's, and... The door. Blood. Stains. Body.

"Suspenders," Nova quivered breathlessly.

"What did he say?" Ruben said.

"Suspenders," Nova repeated.

"He's actually lost it." Ruben threw his arms up and began to pace.

"Okay, Nova. Have a seat." Magenta guided him to the chair by the desk.

Then, turning back to Ruben and Pearl, Magenta shook her head. "I almost got him out, but he keeps going in and out of consciousness."

"What is happening to him?" Pearl whispered.

Seeing Nova in such a state had finally pulled her out of her fears. Unconsciously, she had projected her terror onto Nova. But, seeing him like this...so fragile.

"This is a common response to trauma," Magenta whispered. "He's dissociating."

"What the fuck are we supposed to do?!" Ruben asked aggressively. He was starting to lose his patience. "What is he even saying?!"

"First, you need to calm down," Magenta said sternly, looking him right in the eye. "Your attitude isn't helping."

"Sorry," Ruben said, looking down to the ground.

"Do you remember those boys we saw earlier?"

"Yes. Don't remind me."

"Did you see what they were wearing?"

"No. I was more preoccupied with the fact that there were two creeps staring at us. I'm sorry I didn't have time to see what they were wearing. Haha. Are you serious?"

"Ages ago, two boys went missing."

"I remember," Pearl said.

"The only thing they found was a pair of striped suspenders..." Ruben finished.

"Exactly," Magenta said, meeting both their eyes. "I don't know about you, but I think there is something behind that door. Something that 'Grandpa Bernie' didn't want anyone to find."

Magenta pointed at Nova. "Nova knows something; he saw something he wasn't supposed to. Whatever Grandpa Bernie had down there has left Nova like this. Nova probably wiped the memory from his mind. Our mind often does that shit to protect us from things we can't handle."

"Yeah, I learned about that in psych my first year," Pearl said softly. "Should we call the police? Or an ambulance?"

"The last thing Nova needs is sirens and cops showing up with bright lights. It will send him further into psychosis. They'll probably send him to a psych ward for a week. That won't do anyone any good."

"So, what do you suggest, doctor?" Ruben said sarcastically.

"I say we see what's behind that door."

"What about Nova?" Ruben gestured to him.

Nova was staring off into nothing.

"Well, he doesn't look like he's going to be going anywhere. I say we leave him there, quickly see what Grandpa's got hidden behind that door, and then we'll be back before he even figured out we left."

"Why do we even need to see what's behind that door?" Pearl asked in a small voice.

"Because, Pearl, what if you were right? If you were, that would mean Grandpa Bernie is...what did they call him? Oh yes, the L.A. Love Hunter. Do you know what that would mean?"

Pearl shook her head.

"Dozens of people out there lost their kids to that psycho. From Inglewood to the Valley. They don't even know if their children or loved ones are still fucking alive. Pearl, that was three decades ago. If Grandpa Bernie is the L.A. Love Hunter, it would bring closure to all those families out there who are still wondering if their family member is alive. Just because it doesn't involve you doesn't mean we can just let this go. I won't."

"All right," Ruben said. "Let's get this over with."

"Pearl?"

Pearl hesitated. "I don't know. I think I should stay behind with Nova. What if something happens up here?"

Magenta paused for a moment. "Keep the door open. And call us if something happens."

"Okay," Pearl said timidly. "Don't be too long."

"We won't. In and out. Ready, Ruben?"

Ruben nodded and pulled open the iron door. It was extremely heavy, and he had to use most of his muscles to pull it.

"What the hell. How on earth did the old man do this."

"Maybe he had help..."

Darkness awaited them. They could just make out the stone spiral of a staircase. Magenta turned her flashlight back on and led the way. Pearl watched them both disappear into the shadows of the stairway a second later. Pearl was left in the silence of the cabin. Nova was rocking slightly in his chair, hugging his elbows close to his chest.

Pearl laid a hand on his thigh. "Nova?"

There was no response.

"I know you probably can't hear me in there, but I wanted to let you know that I'm sorry. I'm sorry for not trusting you, and for acting the way I did."

She glanced over at him, but he was still in his dissociated state.

"The truth is, I always liked you...but I was scared. I didn't know what was real and what wasn't. And if there was anyone I would choose to be chased by strange acid ghosts with, it would be you. I guess I'm in too deep and want something to be off about you."

Pearl laughed at the absurdity of what she just said.

"I just wanted you to know that things are going to be different between us when we get through this. *Good* different. That is...if you want things to change..." Pearl put a hand over her face. "God, I'm talking to myself."

Pearl let out a sigh and glanced toward the door. She had to look away almost immediately as a cold shiver snaked through her body. Time passed slowly, and the loud ticking clock in the cabin didn't help at all. After waiting a restless ten minutes, that was more akin to eternity, Pearl paced, splitting her gaze equally between the door and Nova. After another equally torturous ten minutes, Pearl decided to sit herself down again. She reached for the phone in her pocket and jumped as her fingers made contact. For just as she grabbed it, the phone buzzed.

Pearl quickly answered the call.

"Magenta! Where are you? What's going on? I'm starting to freak out here!"

"P-Pearl! Pearl?" The quality of the call was as choppy and fragmented as ocean waves in a storm.

"Magenta? Are you there? Can you hear me?"

"Pearl! I–czh--You're not going to believe this–czh--You need to–czh--Don't come–czh."

"Magenta? Magenta?!"

Pearl was left with a monotone beep as the phone cut out.

"Fuck... Fuck!" Pearl tried calling Magenta with trembling fingers, but it went straight to voicemail.

132

Suddenly, something moved in her peripheral vision, and she felt a vice grip around her arm. She screamed and almost threw her phone across the room. It was Nova. His eyes were wide and terrified.

"Pearl. Where are Magenta and Ruben?"

Pearl tried to pull her arm free.

"They went to see what was behind the door!"

Nova's face lost its color.

"Let go! You're hurting me," Pearl said, trying to pry Nova's fingers from her arm. But Nova didn't let go.

His eyes were darting back and forth in thought, then they stopped and locked onto Pearl's.

"Pearl. Listen to me. Go back to the house. Take photos of everything we found and run."

"What are you talking about? Let go!"

"Did you hear me?! You need to go! And run. Now."

"Okay! Okay! I heard you!"

Nova let his grip on Pearl's arm loosen. She pulled away, looking at Nova, more scared than she had been all night.

"What's going on?"

"Magenta and Ruben are in danger. You need to go now," Nova said calmly, standing up and walking to the door.

"Nova, I don't understand..." She was beginning to tear up.

"Go, Pearl!" Nova screamed.

Tears escaped her eyes and she cowered.

"Go!"

Pearl ran.

Nova clenched his jaw and turned back toward the door like he had become possessed. The shadows whispered dark traitorous voices in his mind. He could hear a woman's heels clacking on concrete and discern his name being called in the faint distance of his consciousness. The tarot card Magenta had pulled earlier burned an image into his mind's eye. He saw the night charging forward with his sword raised and battle cry frozen in the still image of the card. Nova had to take ownership of his memories. He had to take responsibility for his own pain, no matter how much it made him want to run. He did not know what awaited him in the black, but like the Knight of Swords, he would not back down just because fear stood as a gatekeeper between him and doing what was right.

Nova grabbed a crowbar that lay on one of the workshop benches and twirled it in his hand before gripping it tightly, wielding it like a sword. He had been told by countless therapists that the nightmares he had been plagued with ever since he was a child were a result of the trauma from his father and the relationship between his parents. He was told that nightmares manifested in strange fantastical ways to help the mind cope with a painful reality. But now Nova knew that they had no clue what he truly faced or how events were connected. It was time to face the truth. Before he could think, Nova stepped into the darkness, leaving the cabin behind and descending the long stone stairway into the unknown.

CHAPTER NINE

Disclosure

Magenta and Ruben made their way down the staircase, which opened into a long and narrow concrete tunnel that extended endlessly both right and left. They exchanged a long, worried look with one another. They had been expecting something out of the ordinary, a creepy basement or a sex dungeon, but this... This exceeded their expectations. Blue, fluorescent lights lined the walls and began to light up as they walked.

"What the fuck... It looks like some sort of bunker." Ruben was speechless.

The amount of time and money this must have taken to build was unimaginable.

"Which way?"

"What?" Ruben was still in disbelief at what he was seeing.

"Left or right?" Magenta clarified.

"The GPS says right," Ruben mocked.

But the decision was quickly made for them. A sound echoed violently down the left side of the tunnel. Ruben grabbed Magenta's arm. The noise screeched like nails on metal.

"Magenta, there's something down here..." Ruben said in barely more than a whisper.

"I guess we know which way to go now."

Magenta took a step in the direction of the noise, which sounded like a mix of screeching and people chanting.

But Ruben pulled her back. "Woah, woah."

Magenta met his eyes with a fierce glare. "Let go of my arm."

"No! Are you sure we should be doing this?"

Magenta yanked her arm free. "Listen, Ruben, there are always creepy noises. The wind probably just opened a rusty door."

"I've never heard a door sound like that."

Magenta rolled her eyes. "Nova's grandpa is dead. Unless you're scared of ghosts?"

Ruben flushed a little. "Fine."

"You sure? 'Cos it's not too late to chicken out. I'm fine to do this alone." Magenta didn't take her eyes off Ruben's for a second.

"Yes. Yes. I am sure."

Magenta held his gaze for another second, then smiled. "Good. Let's get this over with."

The two began the walk down the tunnel. It must have extended for at least a mile or two because it had been almost twenty minutes.

"Where the fuck are we?"

"Somewhere in the hills...maybe the Burbank side? Under the Hollywood sign?"

They came to a door. There was a keypad beside it. Ruben went for the handle, but it wouldn't budge.

"Jesus... Either Grandpa Bernie was a deluded paranoid about the end of the world, or he had some major secrets."

Magenta ignored Ruben and crouched down to assess the numeric keypad. There were six dashed lines on the display screen.

"It needs a six-digit code," she whispered, thinking out loud to herself.

"Great... How in the hell are we going to figure that out?"

As soon as he said it, a click resonated and the door opened. He stared dumbfounded down at Magenta who was pulling her fingers away from the keypad.

She looked at him and rolled her eyes. "What? I found that number everywhere. It was on Grandpa Bernie's freemason medal. It was in the notes I found in his desk. It also happens to be the date Nova was born in reverse plus the number twenty-two. Stop underestimating me, bro."

"Who are you?"

"Come on, idiot." Magenta opened the door and stepped inside.

"No, seriously," Ruben said, following her. "Are you, like, an undercover detective or something? 'Cause I've seen *21 Jump Street*. Just tell me now if you are. I won't be mad..."

His voice trailed off as he registered what was on the other side of the door. They had stepped into another corridor, except this one was full of doors, each with a glass window looking into dozens of rooms. It was like stepping into an apocalyptic, subterranean hospital.

"What the hell...?"

Magenta was already stepping forward. The first room was empty, except for a single bed. Blue lights flickered inside, illuminating the drawings on the wall in...

"Blood." Magenta's throat suddenly began to get very dry.

"Magenta." Ruben's voice became deadly serious. Like the lingering silence after a fresh cut rose stem. Dread dropped in their chests as they took in what was before them.

"Okay, I think we've seen enough now," Ruben said through a scratched whisper.

But Magenta was opening the door to the first room; her eyes transfixed on the wall. "Magenta!" Ruben yelled as much as a whisper could be yelled.

A rogue breeze skirted along the line of his neck, and he jumped. He swatted at the empty air like he was swatting a fly, and a thin cold sweat seeped from the pores in his skin.

"Fucking hell."

He relented and followed Magenta inside.

The writing on the walls was an amalgamation of strange symbols. As the blue fluorescent light flickered outside the vacant room, it illuminated the symbols in strange shadows. They were written everywhere. Over and over. The same line. Vertically, upside down, on the walls, the floor, the ceiling, like hieroglyphics and tribal symbols. And in the center of the room was a scale, like the old type used to measure spices.

"Judgment..." Magenta whispered. "Just like the cards said."

"What the hell are you talking about?" Ruben's voice quivered.

"The scales... In ancient Egypt, the god of the death Anubis would weigh your heart on a scale and pass judgment on whether you were to be accepted into the afterlife. If you failed..." Her voice trailed off as she recalled the rest of the myth. "You would be thrown into the mouth of the devourer."

"Well, great!" Ruben clapped his hands together. "Can we go now?"

He was disturbed far past his comfort zone, and he had seen a lot of disturbing things in his life.

"We need to see what else is here," Magenta said finally.

"Are you fucking kidding me, Magenta?"

Magenta nudged past him and went back into the hall. Ruben again felt that cold sweat rise on the back of his neck and he followed her, cursing under his breath. There were dozens of doors all along the corridor. This time Magenta moved faster. Each of the rooms was almost the same in appearance; empty except for a bed that was built into the floor itself, like rectangular concrete coffins without lids. However, none of the rooms were as desecrated as the first. After the sixth window, they found something else, though. Drawings. Not in blood but scratched into the wall. They were simple, stick figure drawings. Like those that would be done by a child.

"This is where he brought them," Magenta said softly. Except there was a dark rumble of anger in the underbelly of her voice.

"Yeah, no shit." Ruben was having trouble keeping his cool.

Magenta suddenly turned toward the end of the corridor and broke into a little jog. "What are you doing now!?" Ruben yelled out.

But Magenta didn't answer. She stopped dead in her tracks and pressed herself tightly against a wall. Ruben was looking at her like she had lost her mind, but she gestured to him to do the same. Ruben buried his face in his hands. He was certain she had gone crazy.

"What the hell are you doing... ?!" But his whisper was cut short when he saw what Magenta was looking at through one of the thick glass windows.

Every fiber in Ruben's body froze as he saw what Magenta was staring at. Through a glass window was a giant room. In it were a dozen more of the rooms they had just seen, except these ones were occupied. Occupied by people. And walking from room to room were people in doctor's coats, each of them wearing face masks.

Ruben could not describe the terror he felt at that moment. He grabbed Magenta's hand because she looked just as terrified as him. They had not just stumbled upon a crazy old man's murder den; they had found something entirely beyond that. Magenta took her phone out of her pocket and dialed. Ruben couldn't make sense of the words that were coming out of her mouth, he knew that they needed to get out. He pulled Magenta away from the window and back toward the way they had come. But at that moment, a door opened, and seven men dressed in black combat uniforms appeared at the other end of the corridor. They wore dark masks that obscured every inch of their faces. Magenta dropped her phone as she saw them. This was it. She had done it. She had gone snooping too far into the dark. Every inch of blood drained from her face as the realization of their fate dawned upon her.

* * *

Pearl ran. She ran as fast as possible away from the dark cabin in the woods. The branches scratched at her face and pulled on her hair like old witches' fingers in the Grimm fairy tales. She could hear movement behind her, but she just kept on running. She couldn't hold back the sobs. The sound of Magenta's voice in the night haunted her. Why was this all happening?! Pearl's mind was fierce with panic. The mansion's lights peeked through the trees, and Pearl practically threw herself through the glass door, locking it behind her. She needed to get out. She needed to call for help. She ran up the stairs to get her clothes when a loud shatter came from below.

Pearl's heart dropped in her chest. *No. No. No. This can't be happening.*

She had to hold back the sob of tears, which felt like a thick rope around her throat. There were voices. Pearl ran into the nearest bedroom, searching for a place to hide. She spotted a closet and quickly hid amongst the hanging coats, tucking herself up into a small ball and forcing her own hand over her mouth. With trembling fingers, she pulled out her phone. In hindsight, she should have called the police, but her finger went instinctively to the first number on her starred contacts. Mom.

Pick up. Pick up. Pick up.

There was a soft clicking sound.

"Pearl?" It was her mother's voice.

The voice was weary and tired, which was to be expected given the time of night. The familiarity of her mother's voice had more tears rolling down Pearl's face.

"Pearl, is that you?"

"Yes," Pearl whispered through quivering tears.

"Honey, are you okay? What's wrong?" Her mom's voice suddenly grew more alert.

"I don't know, Mom..." Pearl began to sob. "Something bad is happening. I need you. I don't know what to do."

"Woah, honey. Where are you?"

"I'm at Nova's house. In the hills," she managed to say through stifled tears. "There are people coming to get me. I don't know what to do."

"What people? Pearl, tell me the address now. I'll come and get you."

Pearl heard another voice from the other side of the phone.

"Daddy!"

It was her father's voice.

At that moment, she heard footsteps in the hall outside.

"Mom, help. They're coming. They're going to find me."

"Who's going to find you? Pearl, what's the address? Your father and I are coming right now."

But it was too late. The door to the closet was thrown open.

Pearl screamed in terror as a figure dressed in black pulled her out by her hair.

"No! No! Stop!"

"Pearl!" her mother screamed back. "Pearl! Where are you?!"

"Nova's grandpa..."

"What, hun?"

"His grandpa is L.A. Love Hunter. We found out. It's a cover-up."

Her mother's next words went unheard, and Pearl was dragged from the room kicking and screaming by unmarked black uniforms.

* * *

Nova had remembered everything he had seen. The memories terrified him to his core, but now that he knew Magenta and Ruben had gone down into the basement, he knew he needed to find them. It was a stairway he had seen countless times as a child. A staircase he had talked about with countless child therapists. But he knew the truth now. He was living it. He remembered the strange woman who would appear. A woman who only came at night when Bernie thought Nova was sleeping. After she arrived, his grandpa would disappear for hours on end. When Nova grew into his teenage years, he had just assumed that his grandpa had some sort of mistress. But that was where his memory was incomplete.

Nova ran down the stairway as fast as he could, coming to the long corridor of blue lights. It was like a nightmare coming to life. He knew this corridor. And yet, he had only ever seen it in his dreams. He could hardly breathe, his lungs burning from the descent. He struggled to ground himself as the familiar walls threatened to close in on him. But the walls didn't actually move; they stayed where they were. Nova heard a scream coming from one end of the tunnel, and all his worst fears came hurtling toward the surface. But something greater than his fears rose as well.

An instinct to protect his friends. To protect them from what happens next. Nova broke into a sprint in the direction of the scream. Everything in his body was telling him to turn around and run away. Every nightmare he had as a child came rushing back, but Nova steeled himself and kept running. There was no turning back now. Whatever was on the other side, Nova would face. He had encountered them numerous times before in his own mind, now was nothing different. Except it was. Even Nova didn't know the extent of what lay beneath his grandpa's cabin.

The lights flickered madly as he ran, casting sharp shadows that shouldn't have been there. Flashes of blood and screaming faces danced amongst them, running through a gallery of memories. He was nearing the first room in half the amount of time it had taken Magenta and Ruben. And, as he neared, the lights ahead of him suddenly went out. Starting from the furthest one, they extinguished one by one. The shadows rushed to meet him. Fear seized his legs, and he skidded to a halt just as he was plunged into complete darkness.

* * *

Magenta woke suddenly. Frantic thoughts swirled in her head as she tried to orient herself. How had she gotten here? Where was *here*? A cloth was wrapped tight around her wrists, and she could feel the rough texture already rubbing her wrists raw. She tried to move, and a howling pain tore in her ribs. A huge wave of dizziness almost sent her back into unconsciousness. She had to bite down hard to keep herself from slipping away. She managed to gasp short staccato breaths. Something was broken.

There was no light in the room except for the stars swimming in her vision. The earlier moments slowly trickled in. Of the rooms. Of the bloody walls. Of the people locked like rats in cages. A movement brushed against her arm, and she practically jumped out of her skin, sending another huge shock of pain pounding through her ribs. She could hardly breathe without her lungs pressing against that sharp stabbing feeling. There was another brush against her arm, then a low groaning noise. Magenta froze before recognition was registered.

"Ruben? Ruben?! Is that you?"

"Magenta..."

Ruben was barely conscious. Both had tried to fight their way through the row of armed guards, and Ruben had taken a particularly hard blow to the head, blood still trickling from the gash on his forehead.

"What happened? Where are we?"

"I don't know." Magenta's voice was quivering. Tears streamed from her eyes. "They got us. I..." Whoever they were. She fought through the choke of tears. "I should have listened to you. I never thought..." Her voice trailed off. "What are they going to do to us?"

Ruben tried to hold his head up, but the effort was too much for him. It dangled toward the ground like a puppet with its strings loose. He was still having trouble formulating thoughts. Everything was thick and foggy.

"Someone will find us, right?" Magenta continued talking. "Our parents will know we've gone missing and call the police. They'll trace it all back to here."

Magenta heard a low gurgle coming from Ruben's mouth. At first, she thought he was choking, until she realized it was a laugh. It made her skin crawl.

"Have you lost it?!"

This only made Ruben laugh more, which sent him into a coughing fit.

"I'm sorry," he finally said. But he was still smiling, not that Magenta could see it. "I haven't talked to my parents in years. I was excommunicated."

Magenta frowned in confusion.

"What the hell are you saying?"

"My parents are Mormons. They kicked me out when I was sixteen. I haven't spoken to them or my brothers and sisters since."

Magenta sighed and leaned her head back against Ruben's, which was still too heavy for him to lift.

"Why did you never tell me?"

"I dunno."

There was a long silence.

"If I died today, no one would even care that I was missing."

"I would."

"Don't lie. We've never even chilled alone together. And we only fuck when we're with other people."

"What? And you think that's because I don't like you?" Magenta pursed her lips and shook her head, pulling it away from Ruben's. "I don't remember the last time I saw you sober. You spend all your time hopping from one friendship group to another. The only time you ever call me is when you're fucked up after a night out. So don't project your bullshit onto me, Ruben. You're the one who's been a bad friend."

There was a long silence. Magenta's teeth were pressed firmly together as she fought back the waves of emotion. Way to make being prisoners in a psycho-killer dungeon even worse.

Ruben suddenly spoke, cutting through the silence. "You're right."

Magenta felt the weight of his emotions in her own chest. She sighed.

"We're going to get out of this," Magenta said. "I don't know how, but Nova will help us. And when we do, we'll go out properly."

Ruben smirked. "Now I have something to look forward to."

Their hands were tied together behind their backs, and Magenta laced her fingers as best she could with Ruben's. A sorrowful lump formed in her chest, but she pushed it away almost as soon as it appeared. If these were going to be her last moments, she sure as hell wouldn't waste them feeling sorry for herself. She and Ruben had danced around their strange relationship for a long time. At least now they were finally facing the feelings they had been ignoring for so long; Magenta just wished they had more time.

* * *

Nova was walking down the empty hallway, the same hallway he had seen a thousand times in his nightmares. He could hear muffled voices coming from the other end. Nova ducked behind a pillar and listened to the echo of footsteps. He frowned as he tried to discern their direction. They seemed to be getting closer and further away at the same time, probably something to do with the acoustics. Nova poked his head briefly around the corner and shot back instantly, doing his best to keep his breathing quiet.

A man in what looked to be a black SWAT uniform was walking directly toward him. Had the man seen him? Nova squeezed his eyes shut. How could this be happening? How was this real? He wished more than anything that this was just another nightmare he could wake up from. But even as he had the thought, he knew daylight would never offer the sweet relief it had before. They had never been nightmares. They had been memories and tenebrous premonitions this entire time. And now his friends were dragged into it, all because Nova had refused to face the truth.

There came the scratch of radio static, and he could hear the man speaking into a communication device. "We got two of them," came his voice. "Still no sign of Crenshaw."

Nova's heart seized. He ignored the latter statement for the prior. Ruben and Magenta... Nova surged with rage. Whoever these people were, they couldn't do this. They couldn't take his friends and get away with it. Nova's next action didn't come out of methodic thought; it came out of instinct.

He swung around the corner of the pillar he was hiding behind just as the guard was stepping up to it. Nova charged and swung the crowbar straight for the guard's head, but instead of the hard thud that he was expecting,

152

Nova heard a soft *thwap.* The man had caught the crowbar mid-swing.

"There you are," the guard said menacingly before kicking Nova square between his legs.

Nova felt the wind shoot out of his lungs in an instant as he went sprawling square onto his back. He quickly tried to scramble away, all the while choking and coughing for air, his winded lungs failing to draw enough.

The guard stood over him like a looming shadow, not slightly threatened by Nova's presence. The guard reached for his radio. "Found him. He was hiding in the corridor. Tell the boss."

"Copy that."

Nova managed to draw in a breath. The crowbar had fallen to the floor and laid by the guard's feet.

"Who-who are you people?" Nova said, trying to hold the guard's attention.

"Save your voice, Crenshaw," the guard replied. "You're lucky the boss wants you unharmed. You're pissin' me off."

Nova swallowed a heavy lump in his throat. "Your boss, what was her name?"

"Enough questions," the guard replied.

Nova stole a quick glance at the crowbar. It was just out of his arm's reach.

"She wants me unharmed, doesn't she? She probably won't be very happy with you if she finds me pinned to the ground."

The guard didn't reply but seemed to shift uncomfortably as if mulling the scenario in his head.

"If you let me up, I will come willingly. You can take me to her yourself."

The guard took a moment before nodding. "Get up!" He gestured with a hand.

Nova went to stand up, then pretended to wince in pain. "Ow. I think you broke my ribs." He feigned his injury and stumbled back down to his hands and knees.

The guard cursed and bent down to help Nova up, but just as he did, Nova took his opportunity. He dashed for the crowbar and seized the cold metal in his hand. In one swift motion, he spun around and swung as hard as he could at the guard's knee. There was a loud cracking sound, and the man let out a holler of pain, collapsing to the ground.

"Not today, you little bitch!"

Judging by the sound his knee made, which was like a plastic water bottle crumpling, there was no doubt that the guard's kneecap had shattered. Nova had a strange realization that reality was not like the movies, where enemies and heroes alike could take endless strikes and punches, even fly through walls, and still get up. The guard would not be standing anytime soon, if ever.

Nova stood above him, wielding the crowbar in a shaking stance above his head, ready to strike again like he had discovered his inner Hulk. He could hardly believe what he had done. He was not a violent person. He had been beaten up multiple times and never thrown a single punch back. He had simply taken the beating and cried about it to his mother later.

Despite not being violent, Nova had to fight with the instinct to end the man right there. A single blow to the head would do it. But Nova couldn't bring himself to act. He lowered his arm, drawing in ragged breaths. Instead, he grabbed the guard's radio and yanked it free from his vest. He couldn't risk the man calling for backup, although the guard's screams had probably already alerted someone. Nova turned around, leaving the man there to writhe in pain, and continued onwards down the corridor, toward where he had heard the other voices coming from mere minutes ago.

As Nova walked away, the man's screaming died out. He had probably passed out from the pain. He craned his neck to confirm. The man lay motionless on the ground. Nova blinked and shook off the blurriness that was starting to swim around the borders of his vision. There was no time to tune out.

Nova didn't know exactly what he would be dealing with as he continued forward. He passed the dimly lit rooms that lined the corridor, peeking his head around each corner to ensure nothing was hiding. But he quickly found out that the only shadow was his own, cast at odd angles by the dim light flickering on the ceiling.

At this point, he considered turning around. Would he really be able to handle what was awaiting him up ahead? He was barely a man. Surely the LAPD would be able to handle things better than he could. But even as he thought it, he realized it was a stupid idea. Whoever these people were, they had resources. *What did you get yourself tied up in, Grandpa?*

Nova took another step forward, and suddenly, all the ceiling lights went out. Nova froze, and his breath became more audible. He had to struggle to mask it, stifling his mouth with a hand as his eyes desperately sought anything to lock onto. Then a single light turned on not six feet away from him.

There came the sound of footsteps. Loud footsteps, unlike the ones from the booted guard. Loud like the clack of high heels on concrete. At that moment, a woman emerged from the shadows on the other side of the spotlight. Spikes of fear struck like daggers in Nova's stomach. He had seen this woman before. She wore a pair of dark crimson heels and a tight-fitting black gown that only draped down one side of her body, revealing a long, toned leg. The first thing that Nova thought when he saw her was that she was beautiful, terrifyingly beautiful, with a subtle, barely detectable seduction. Her eyes were sharp emerald knives plucked straight from a serpent. Her very presence seemed to be a rattled warning.

"Hello, Nova." Her voice was smooth and icy, like the hollow chamber of a 45-millimeter gun. "It's a shame we have to meet in such circumstances. I was looking forward to seeing the look on your face when I turned up on your doorstep. Although I can't say I'm disappointed by what I see now."

"Who are you?" Nova managed to utter through the cold press of fear. He wielded the crowbar shakily, preparing to strike her at any moment.

"You know who I am, Nova. You've known for a long time."

"No... I..." Nova struggled to speak.

"My name is Francesca Bizarr." She held out an elegant hand. "But we've met before. You do remember, don't you? It almost seems like a lifetime ago."

Nova stared at her outstretched hand, focusing all his energy on keeping himself from trembling. When she saw that he wasn't making any move to shake her hand, she withdrew it and propped her elbow on her forearm, pointing at Nova with one finger.

"You remind me of your grandfather, actually. It was such a shame to lose him. He really did a lot for us. Actually, now that I see you in the light, you have that same intense look in the back of your eyes. Of determination! And purpose! I understand why he chose you to take care of his estate and not that fool of a son he had."

A memory flickered in the back of Nova's mind. He had been playing with a model airplane when Francesca appeared in the house beside his grandfather and Lennox. Nova looked at her like she was a queen straight out of some of the stories he had read. Francesca had smiled and kneeled, pulled a dark red lollipop out of her purse, and handed it to him. Bernie had cut their interaction short, and before Nova knew it, he was watching them all walk away into Bernie's office.

Nova swallowed a heavy lump in his throat as he stared at her now. She looked the same as when he had last seen her when he was a child. She hadn't aged a day. He remembered the High Priestess card from earlier in the night. This woman was the spitting image of power, and in her eyes, she held secrets that Nova desperately wanted to uncover. And as if she were reading his mind, she smiled and beckoned him forward.

"Why don't you follow me? I want to show you something."

Nova shook his head, keeping his feet planted firmly on the ground and raising the crowbar even higher. Nova knew that whatever happened from this point out would be a test. He didn't know what game she was playing, but if he made one wrong move, it could mean the end of him, or worse, the end of his friends. Francesca could feel Nova contemplating striking her over the head.

"Oh, please, Nova. You wouldn't hurt a woman," she said softly. "I mean you no harm, nor your friends. What happens to them is up to you."

She turned, and the lights in the tunnel flickered back on, one by one. She walked forward, her high heels echoing against the concrete floor. But Nova didn't move a muscle. He clenched his fists and stayed rooted right where he was. He didn't know where this woman was going or what she wanted to show him, but he knew in the very marrow of his bones that it was not good.

"Where are my friends?" he asked through gritted teeth.

She stopped and turned slightly at the sound of his voice. "They are safe. For now."

"Excuse me if I have trouble believing anything you say."

Francesca raised an eyebrow, then a sly smile formed in the right corner of her mouth. "You really do remind me so much of your grandfather."

Nova ignored the statement. "Take me to them."

Francesca's smile dropped. "I am sorry to burst your bubble, Nova, but you're not the one that calls the shots around here."

Nova heard footsteps behind him and turned to see a line of men in combat uniforms approaching him. Behind the row were another two men carrying the barely conscious guard that Nova had crippled. But Nova's eyes widened when he noticed a body slung over one of the men's shoulders.

"Pearl!"

Nova rushed toward her, but two men broke away from the line and seized him before he got close enough.

"She can't hear you," Francesca said from behind him as Nova struggled and fought against the men holding him back. "We made sure she wasn't harmed, but we couldn't have word getting out about what goes on around here."

Nova clenched his jaw as the men forced him to face Francesca.

"You have a decision to make, Nova. Right now, the lives of your friends are in your hands, so I would tread very carefully."

"Who are you people?" Nova asked, breathless from the struggle.

The smile returned to Francesca's face. "I'm so happy you asked."

Nova was led down the tunnel. Room after room began to appear, and Nova could only stare in dread at what must have gone on within those walls. He thought of the bodies. Of the suspenders... Of his friends. The weight of guilt pressed on him as the soldiers continued to push him onwards. Eventually, they reached the end of the tunnel, and Francesca used a keycard to open the door that stood there. Nova stared at it like it was Pluto's Gate, one of the fabled entrances to the underworld. He expected to find a river of souls with a flimsy boat meant to carry him onwards to judgment. But this was not the underworld. It was worse.

"You can let go of him now," Francesca said to the armed men. "I'll take it from here."

Ghostly faces stared at Nova from behind glass encasements of prison rooms. Some looked human. Others... Nova's mind began to jitter and skip, almost like a glitch in the matrix, struggling to accept what he saw before him.

"Welcome to Agartha, Nova. We have been called many things; a secret society, a cult, bladiblah." She waved her hand. "At the core, we are protectors. Pioneers. Crusaders of a different kind, on a special mission to locate and capture *intra*terrestrial...beings...that have come to infiltrate our way of life."

Nova locked eyes with a human-looking boy. Well, everything about him looked human except for his eyes. They were narrow slits, just like those of a reptile. Nova couldn't believe what he was seeing. All the rooms formed a circle around one giant central room filled with computers and monitors and humans in white lab coats. He looked up and saw that there were at least seven more levels almost identical to the first. Rings of rooms rose within the subterranean base.

The boy with the reptilian eyes flicked his head at Nova, and as he did, his skin shimmered. Nova watched with horror as the molecules of his skin began to rearrange in a scale-like pattern. In the next moment, Nova was staring at his own face.

"No... No, this can't be real."

"Ahh, I see you've met Igor. We picked him up in a rural part of Russia. The farmers had dug up an old myth. They called him a *Skin Walker*. Rather disconcerting, wouldn't you say? He murdered about fifty people before we caught him. Ate them alive, slowly drawing their blood before changing into them and wearing their skin, in a manner of speaking. Would have been a hard cookie to spot if it weren't for those eyes."

Nova stared at a perfect copy of himself, almost like he was looking in a mirror, except for the eyes. They still had that narrow-slit reptilian glaze, emotionless and unreadable. Francesca continued to walk, and the guards pressed Nova on, pushing him forward with the butts of their guns.

"You see, we are not alone. Far from it, actually," she continued. "There are hundreds, if not thousands, of these...abominations living amongst us. Some come from distant star systems, others from a different dimension altogether. Most from within and below. We were tasked with capturing these creatures."

Francesca carefully observed Nova's expression. "Can you imagine if the public found out their worst nightmare was true? Imagine living a lifetime praying to whatever it is they pray to, only to find out...there's more. Right under your feet. The implications. Oh, not to mention they're breeding with humans."

Nova shook his head as they continued walking, trying his best to ignore the people inside the glass prisons. "Why are you showing me all this?"

162

Francesca stopped and turned to face him.

"Your grandfather was instrumental in the progress of our mission. His research on genetics revolutionized our understanding of the true reason behind humanity's evolution. You should be very proud. Without him, none of this would have been possible. Your bloodline is crucial to achieving our goal. Your ancestors were our leaders."

Nova was shaking his head, and his entire body started to tremble. He was going into shock again.

"Don't worry, Nova. All of this will make a lot more sense in just a moment. You are not in any danger."

"P-please..." He managed to stutter. "My friends."

Pearl was still unconscious, and he watched as she was taken to one of the empty rooms and dumped like a rag doll onto the bed.

"Like I said, they will be safe too–if you are willing to cooperate with us. You are smart enough to see that we can't have word about this getting out to the public."

"What do you want from me?"

"Follow me."

Francesca clicked her fingers, and two scientists opened the door to the central room. Francesca's heels clacked loudly against the floor as she walked.

"Come on, Nova," she said without turning. "I want to introduce you to the team."

Nova's emotions were a dark bundle of horror. He kept expecting to wake up and find that this was all some sort of sick dream. But the longer he remained in this underground world, the more he realized that his entire life had just spun into an irretrievable hell. He forced his body to move, to follow Francesca into the giant room filled with computers and scientists.

"Everyone, this is Nova Crenshaw."

The scientists stood and applauded as Nova entered.

What the hell is going on?!

"Bernie's death was a great weight upon us all. But his bloodline lives on. Nova here will carry us forward," Francesca continued.

The applause broke into a cheer.

Nova stared blankly at the strange display presented to him and was literally at a loss for words.

"Okay. That's enough for the introduction." Francesca raised her hands with a big smile on her face. "We don't want to overwhelm the boy. This must be a lot. Back to work. We'll all meet again when Nova has been properly oriented."

The scientists smiled as they resumed their work.

Francesca turned to Nova. "Please excuse them. You're somewhat of a celebrity here."

"I don't understand. What the hell is all this?" Nova's throat was dry and cracked as he spoke.

"Come with me." Francesca walked forward, redirecting her attention to two scientists that seemed to be on standby, awaiting her instructions. "Prepare the neural implant," she whispered to them.

"Implant?" Nova wondered to himself.

The scientists broke off a moment later, disappearing from the room and out of sight.

"Your grandfather and my father Lennox built this from the ground up."

"Everything you see here is the culmination of now two generations worth of hard work. The implant will get you up to speed."

The words that came out of her mouth fell flat of any meaning. They passed straight through one of Nova's ears and out the other. All Nova could think about was Pearl alone in that room and Ruben and Magenta. He had no clue where they were. As if sensing his state of mind, Francesca stopped talking. She met his eyes with what resembled empathy.

"I know you must be worried about your friends. I am going to be honest with you; your friends cannot return to the surface. Not without certain...insurances. The best course would be to give them a role here. Provide them with a purpose so they can live out their remaining years. Humans do better when their purpose is clear. And outlined."

Her words were like lead dropped in water. They sank to the very pit of Nova's stomach. What the hell was that supposed to mean?

The reality began to set in. If he wanted his friends and himself to survive, he would have to follow along with whatever sick game was being played here. He would have to do everything Francesca said.

She turned around and looked Nova up and down, no doubt both sensing and seeing the shock and horror on his face. Her expression turned from upbeat to empathetic. Turning to her guards, she snapped her fingers and waved them off.

"Leave us. I need a moment alone."

The guards reluctantly let Nova go and took a couple of steps back. Francesca opened a door and stood patiently, gesturing for Nova to go in before her. He clenched his jaw and did as he was told. Inside was a bare room with a desk and two chairs. Francesca followed him in and closed the door behind her. She pulled out a chair and gestured for him to sit, walking around the table, and taking a seat for herself on the opposite side.

Nova stood for a second, hovering, assessing the situation. Francesca merely waited, interlacing her fingers and crossing one leg over the other, nonchalantly dangling a heel. Nova watched as her heel bobbed up and down, revealing a dark stockinged arch. He took in a deep breath and sat down opposite her.

"Look, Nova," she said frankly, leaning toward him a little and staring right into his eyes. Nova gulped. *God, her eyes were beautiful.* "I know you didn't ask for this, and I wish that we could have met in different circumstances. You were not supposed to find us like this, nor were your friends ever meant to be involved. But here we are."

166

It was the voice of reason, sympathy, and kindness. Nova found it disconcerting that she could switch so quickly.

"I was actually waiting for you to have lived your life a little more. Graduate college, see what the world was really like first..." Her voice trailed off. "Your grandfather was a great man, and he did things for this planet that deserve medals and honors beyond anything our country is capable of handing out." She paused and gestured around with her hands. "This is all your grandfather's legacy. His real legacy. It's not the money or the mansion; it's the work. Work is all that matters, do you understand?"

Nova sat in silence as she spoke. He found that her words had an eerie way of calming him down. He struggled to fight it, but all he needed to do was remind himself of Pearl. Of Ruben and Magenta. Francesca looked at him and extended a hand toward him. When her skin touched his, there was a sort of electrical charge. Nova pulled away instinctively.

She smiled and sat back. "I know this has all been a little...much. But, trust me, if you give me a chance, I would love to show you what your grandfather has left for you. This is a chance to not only be a part of something real and *actually* work for something that matters, but also the work you will do here will move the needle forward and save lives." She paused, her eyes glazing over as if remembering something. Then she smirked. "Your grandfather had a nickname here. You want to know what it was?"

Nova didn't say anything.

"The Silent Ranger." She raised her eyebrows. "Has a superhero ring to it, don't you think?"

Nova ignored her. "What do I need to do?"

She tipped her head, looking slightly puzzled.

"What do I need to do to save Pearl, Magenta, and Ruben? They aren't involved in this, right?"

Francesca clasped her elegant hands together and sighed. "Nova, there is no sweet way to put this. Your friends won't be leaving here. Now, under the right circumstances, we can give them a place and a function among us, and if things go well and genuine trust is earned, they may one day gain the freedom to return to the outside world. Under our supervision, of course. I wish I could tell you we had a device that could erase all this from their memory, but this isn't the *Men in Black*."

Nova found his fists were clenched in his lap under the table, and so was his jaw. He shook his head.

"You know, I used to think I was living in a delusion, and for the most part, I was. But now that I've met you, I see that you're living in an even bigger one. Do you really expect me to go along with this? To be happy and accept my grandfather's fucked up inheritance. I was happy with the cars and the mansion."

"No, you weren't." Francesca's expression turned harder. "Take a good long look at your life, Nova. Tell

168

me of a moment–just one–where you were truly happy. Go on."

Nova went to speak, then found himself stopping short. He frowned and scanned his memories for anything to prove her wrong.

"Are you happy being on Zoloft? Are you happy with addict parents?"

Nova's demeanor changed subtly.

"And let's face it...no one cares about a black man's happiness. Did you forget that?"

Nova could feel Francesca manipulating him, but it was hard for him to not be triggered by her words.

"You see, when I met your grandfather, he was already rich. But he wasn't happy either. He was full of greed and abused his power, taking out most of his anger and frustrations on your father, might I add. That all changed when he started his work here. The Bernie you knew was a result of this. A result of his work *here*." She leaned forward again. "Purpose, Nova. Purpose is at the core of every human being, and without it, we are only shadows of our higher selves. Purpose is what drives all our goals and values; it is the root of what it means to be alive. And a man without purpose..."

"...isn't a man." Francesca shrugged apologetically.

"I never asked for this..." Nova replied.

"You're right. Leaders never ask; the role is bestowed upon them. A king is born into their birthright. No matter how hard they try to fight it, the crown will someday be placed upon their head."

Tears began to pool in Nova's eyes. Not for himself but for his friends. He imagined them stuck in this dark place, void of any sunlight or fresh air. Slaves. That was what they would be. But as the tears began to well, he once again remembered the card that Magenta had pulled— The Knight of Swords. He remembered the fierce charge with the raised sword. Nova was not that Knight, but he could learn to be.

He saw how every card Magenta pulled had come to fruition, and the last one hit harder than he could have ever known. The Tower. A card that pulled life from beneath him, like a carpet, yanking and turning the whole world upside down.

Nova stopped the tears from streaming. He steeled his heart and visualized himself upon the steed, wielding the sword, ready to cut through anything that stood in his path. If he wanted his friends to survive, he would need to get them out of here. No one else could do that for them apart from him. Nova looked up and met Francesca's eyes with a deep severity, and he smiled.

"Okay," he said.

Francesca raised her eyebrows in surprise and met his gaze with a snake-like smile of her own.

"I will take up my grandfather's legacy. I will join Agartha."

Francesca was a woman who played games. Nova knew that whatever she had planned here, she had already planned a thousand different scenarios into the future. She was the kind of person who was always a hundred steps ahead of everyone else. It would not be easy, but Nova would learn to be better than her. He would play along for as long as it took, and he would find a chink in her armor. Even if his friends hated him for the rest of their lives, he would do everything in his power to free them.

Francesca rose from her seat, and Nova mirrored the action. Instead of shaking his hand, Francesca stepped right up to him. She was as tall as him, and she stared into his eyes. Her scent was intoxicating at such close quarters. It was like a siren's song, a hazard masked in beauty and fragrance. She grazed a long-nailed finger over his face and stepped past him, opening the door and heading into the main hall.

"We need to show you what your ancestors accomplished," she said softly as Nova fell into step alongside her. "The key to why you are so important is in your genetics, Nova." She glanced at him from the corner of her eyes. "They must be activated so your ancestors' memories may live on."

Nova followed her as a hard resolve settled in his heart. In a single moment, Nova had changed. He would no longer be the coward on the sandbox pummeled by the bullies. He would no longer be the antidepressant pill-popping sob story he was before. Francesca was right. A man did need a purpose, and Nova had found one. But it was not the one Francesca intended. No doubt she knew his real intentions; she was smarter than anyone he had ever met, with a gaze that could penetrate any lie. But, if the strength of a man was weighed by his reason to live, then Nova knew he was stronger. Strength was more powerful than wit.

She opened another door where three scientists stood waiting. In the center of the room was Nova's legacy, a legacy wrapped in steel and machinery Nova hadn't the mind to understand. He took a deep breath and brandished the imaginary sword in his hand, stepping forward and allowing the scientists to strap him in. Thinking of his friends the whole time and already beginning to plan how he would outsmart the High Priestess.

"Prep the neural implant," Francesca requested.

Nova gulped.

TO BE CONTINUED IN

GRANDPA'S CABIN
BOOK 2

ABOUT THE AUTHOR

Ross Victory is a singer/songwriter and award-winning author from Southern California.

After the loss of his father and brother, Ross dove into self-discovery, reigniting his childhood passion for writing and music production. Victory has dedicated his life to empowering the creative community while inspiring and entertaining listeners and readers. Victory provides a multi-format creative experience in Urban Adult Contemporary music and literature, with a focus on creative non-fiction and novellas.

Victory is best known for his father-son memoir, "Views from the Cockpit," and his brand, "Books & Bangers."

ALSO AVAILABLE

★ ★ ★ ★ ★

"I'm overwhelmed by the *gorgeous* language..."
- Writer's Digest, Nicole Howard

"...Victory is a talented writer"
- Penguin Random House, Michael McConnell

"...courageous words from a Black man..."
- African American Literature Book Club, Robert Fleming